All The Best

....

Miryam Sila

Copyright © 2023 by Miryam Sila

All rights reserved.

No portion of this book may be reproduced in any form without written permission from the publisher or author, except as permitted by U.S. copyright law.

Contents

----

1 - Delilah	1
2 - Mason	8
3 - Delilah	16
4 - Delilah	25
5 - Mason	31
6 - Delilah	40
7 - Delilah	46
8 - Mason	54
9 - Delilah	61
10 - Mason	71
11 - Delilah	78
12 - Mason	86
13 - Delilah	92
14 - Mason	99
15 - Delilah	107

16 - Delilah	115
17 - Mason	122
18 - Delilah (before)	129
19 - Delilah	135
20 - Mason	141
21 - Delilah	148
22 - Mason	156
23 - Mason	164
24 - Delilah	170
25 - Mason	177

1 - Delilah

"So, you wanna head back to my place?"

I tell myself to smile, and look bashfully excited. He's asking to take me home, which translated to—can I take you home and fuck you on the first date? I tell myself to appear like the single sentence didn't disgust me and instantly decide my plans for the night—all of which did not include him.

I flash him a smile and pick up my almost-empty wine glass. "I have an early morning tomorrow. I'm sorry but I can't." Just smile Del, just smile. I hate that I apologized for saying that I can't come over but the worry that I might upset him and result in a scene lingered in the back of my mind. Along with the worry, all the horror stories that I've heard and seen when women reject men, are terrifying.

I watch the instant my words reach his brain and he realizes I'm not interested in sleeping with him tonight. As if I owed him some sort of favor and he expected me to just oblige. I specifically stated in our Tinder DMS that I am not interested in a hookup— apparently, he didn't get the memo.

"Oh." Disappointment is clear as he speaks. I turn my attention to the white napkin folded in my lap, picking it up and dabbing the corners of my mouth. The restaurant we had decided on was on the nicer side of the city. I took it as an opportunity to dress up for once, settling on my favorite red dress. It looks a little different on my adult body than it did all those years ago in undergrad, but I felt good nonetheless. What a waste it was tonight.

"I'm sorry, I gotta run. This was fun, Sam." His rushed movements cause me to drop my napkin and ignore the urge to roll my eyes at his lack of remembering my name. "You got the bill, right? I'm a little short on cash lately. Catch ya later." Tim, who works in marketing and is far too cocky for his own good, stands and grabs his jacket from the chair. Not only did the douchebag not remember my name, but he was also leaving me to pay the bill in full alone.

And they say chivalry is dead.

I nod silently knowing if I spoke I'd just cause a scene.

He flees the restaurant like his ass is on fire, people are too busy to notice except for our waitress who makes her way over tentatively, "Everything okay here, miss?"

I grip the corner of the table, tilting my head up to respond, "Yes. Just the bill please."

She nods her head, face full of understanding of what had just happened. Yes, I just got left at the table on a first date. Yes, it's because I didn't throw him a bone that I'd like to sleep with him and his potentially very sad attempt at making me cum. I'm twenty-five years old, too old to be going home with random men who only want to get in my pants. I should've known better than trying to give a man on Tinder the benefit of the doubt. Never again.

So I just smile up at her, silently asking her to leave and get the bill so my straight facade can break. What's one more bad date? It's not as if I'd been trying to get back into the dating scene for months now. I already had a handful of dating horror stories that I'm sure would get a crowd going, what's one more to add to it?

I pay the bill, all one hundred and thirty dollars worth plus tip, and high-tail it out of this place.

The second I reach the street I unlock my phone that's been silently buzzing all night with texts from what I can only assume is my girl's group chat. Ignoring the millions of messages and unanswered questions I open the ride-share app and order a car to my favorite bar—Old Joe's.

The September night air had me wishing I had opted for that coat on the way out tonight instead of this thin cardigan that was no real barrier. I could've at least used it as a comforting hug right now, god knows I need one.

"Miss, are you alright?" The same waitress from inside steps up beside me. She's a little bit shorter than I am but that's not unusual with my 5'9 height.

"Yes, I am. Thank you for checking on me." I sincerely say.

"I just want you to know men are absolute trash and I'm so sorry that fool left you." She shakes her head, her long braids flowing over her shoulder. "I swear I've seen it more times than I'd like and it's never not disappointing." She turns to face me now and I notice that she's got her bag and coat, so I assume she's just got off.

"It's okay. I've been through worse in life than a man dining and dashing because he wasn't getting his dick wet." I laugh with her at my own words and the sound is a welcoming one to my dampened mood.

"Well, this is my ride," I step forward pointing to the car with the same license plate as the one on my phone. "Thank you again for everything." I wave while sliding into the back seat. The waitress, whose name I remember as Jordyn from the receipt, waves back and wishes me goodnight.

Now if only all people were as kind as her, then maybe just maybe I'd have better luck with life. It seems as though whenever I am at my wit's end with my current life, the universe turns a rough patch into a gaping hole and I step right through.

But I wouldn't let one loser ruin my night, no. It was my first weekend off since back to PA school and I would most definitely be using this as an opportunity to get shit-faced like I was 21 for the first time again. My twenty-one and twenty-five-year-old self were completely different and on very different paths in life. One of them almost got married and the other was getting left on first dates. Thoughts of perfect smiles, two dimples, and a mop of brown wavy hair infiltrated my mind and it got harder to breathe for a moment.

The only feelings associated with memories like those were heartbreak and pain, two of which I refused to deal with tonight. I've had enough of that to go around for a while.

"Here we are." The driver stops the car in front of the packed bar. I thank him for the drive and step out, back into the unforgiving night air. Luckily there is no line to get in, which is rare these days and usually only happens when capacity is at an all-time high.

Old Joes had been the town of Portsneck's pride and joy for years. When I was younger and just old enough to drive, I had picked my mother and father up many times at this spot. I could picture it now, my mother hanging off the shoulder of my dad too consumed with laughter from a joke told by a local just inside the bar, to walk straight.

You never realize what you take for granted until it's gone. Thoughts of my mother's smile and my father's undying love for her nailed me in the chest. I tried to remind myself coming here was for a break from the sad date and not an opportunity to feel sad about myself.

Showing the bouncer my ID, I was welcomed inside by the sights and sounds of the local nightlife. There was a state college just ten minutes away where the bar got most of its crowd from, most of them in their early twenties or most likely under twenty-one with a fake ID in their back pockets. I helped myself to a seat at the bar, breathing in the familiar stale air and flagging down the bartender Joe.

"If it isn't my favorite loyal customer." Joe always cast a warm smile my way whenever I had the pleasure of being in his presence.

"Don't start making me sound like an alcoholic Joe." I tease, knowing that's entirely impossible considering I can count on one hand how many times I've gone out in the last year and a half.

"Never Darlin," he slid a beer my way. "But I did know your mother, and she loved these." He points to the dripping glass and I shake my head.

"Thank you." I smile, already feeling the weight of my awful date leaving my shoulders. I took a sip of the cold draft beer and let myself relax for the first time tonight.

When I agreed to go out with the Tinder guy, I thought it would be a nice break from the consistent studying I had been doing leading up to my first exam. He seemed nice enough and not like a complete douche who was just trying to get in my pants, or else I would've never agreed. I couldn't even say that at least I had gotten a free meal out of it, how sad.

"Lonely girl at a bar, dressed in red and drinking a cold beer. What fool left you tonight?" I turn my head to the intruder to my right. The first thing I notice about him is how tall he is, and the second thing I notice is the ring finger on his left hand. I relax for a moment, hoping that he's just being friendly.

"You don't want to know." I give him a nod of my head while sipping my beer.

He flashes me a white smile and shakes his head. "If my wife was here she'd have something inspirational to say or some shit but I'm not good at all that." I pick up on the wife part and drop my guard, knowing he's not trying to hit on me.

"That's okay. I think I'll just enjoy this beer." I shake the drink in my hand. "What brings you to Portsneck?" I ask, wondering why I have never seen him around before. I wouldn't say the town is small but it's not large and I have seen at least everyone in the town once before.

"A friend of mine is visiting his family before we head back up to the city for the first of our season." He nods to a group of guys to our left and I lean back a bit on the stool to see who he's pointing at and almost fall flat on my back.

Standing there in all his 6'5, brown curly hair, glory is Mason Jones. In that one small second of seeing his profile, I was transported four years back when the man across the bar was more than just a stranger. My heart drops and I lose focus for a moment, a moment too long because the stool I sit on starts to slip. I yelp, completely startled but the man next to me whose name I never got, grips my arm to prevent me from falling.

I need to get out of here immediately.

I already feel the effects of seeing Mason for the first time in years. The sweaty palms, heavy breathing, and anxiety creeping up my chest are all too familiar feelings when thinking about my very real ex-boyfriend.

"Thank you," I say breathlessly. I drop a twenty on the bar top, my hands shaking. Suddenly I'm that nineteen-year-old girl again who loves too big and falls too fast. All the memories good and bad start crashing back and forth through my head like the waves of the ocean and I stand quickly.

"Are you alright?" The guy next to me stands, worry on his face at my frazzled form.

"Yes I am, I just remembered I have somewhere to be. Enjoy your time here and thank you again for saving me from some serious embarrassment." I laugh to lighten the strange mood. He nods his head and doesn't get the opportunity to say anything because I'm already rushing out of there.

Mason is back.

That thought alone has me struggling to breathe and I've never been more thankful all night that I didn't bring a jacket because as soon as I step outside the frigid air is a welcoming wake-up call.

"Delilah?" Oh no, oh fuck.

I know that voice too well. It sends an all too familiar feeling of butterflies to my stomach and reminds me of a time when life looked a lot different than it does now. It pains me to turn around, but I do it very slowly.

"Holy shit, it is you."

2 - Mason

"Coach says we gotta be back by Monday morning for drills."

Darius points to an email he has pulled up on his phone. I drop the towel from my hands, ignoring the sweat dripping from my forehead for a moment to read the entire message. Our season starts in two weeks and we're practicing and training as hard as ever. We're about to be on the road and in new cities for new games every week for the rest of the year, so we're allowed one weekend at home before the circus starts.

"Should be fine. I'm just going to see my Dad and then catch up with some hometown friends." I finish wiping the sweat from my forehead. "What about you? Spending it with your wife?" I assume Darius would be spending the weekend with his girl considering they just tied the knot early this year.

"She's coming on the road with me, remember? I'm going to take you up on your offer from before and come home with you." He slaps my back with a laugh. "Time to see where the golden boy grew up." I shake my head at his teasing that he and all the others like to join in on while slapping his hand away from my back.

"It's nothing exciting. I can promise you it's the least exciting thing you'll see." Standing from the metal bench I stretch my arms across my chest, wincing at the feeling of soreness. Working my upper body was my favorite type of workout but it always got to me.

"See you in the AM." He's dressed and ready to go, stepping in front of me and tapping his hat as he passes. I wave him goodbye and pick up my shit thrown everywhere before heading out to the car. I still need to pack for tomorrow's drive down to Portsneck so I ditch my original plans of meeting up with some of the team for dinner and just head straight back to my apartment.

...

"I bet you ten bucks you won't make it one night without hooking up with a local fan." Darius teases me as we step out of the car that's just dropped us off at my Dad's place.

"Stop making me out to be a fuckboy D, you know that's not me." I shake his hand off my back and grin widely. "I'll at least wait until tomorrow night." I joke. He laughs at my response and follows me up the steps to my family home.

I rarely come back here, the memories are sometimes too much too bare. I chose to spend my free time focusing on my game or hitting the bars with the team. I throw myself completely into forgetting everything there is to do about this town and everyone in it.

"Mason! You made it!" My stepmother greets me with a wide hug. I tense the second her arms surround me and awkwardly pat her back.

I've never been good with touch. I don't know why or how but over the last few years I've grown more and more animosity toward touching and any sort of affection. The feeling of someone's hands or arms around my body sends straight panic and disgust to my brain. It makes my dating life and sex life almost non existent.

I immediately stepped back from her arms as quickly as they came around me. "Good to see you, Marie," I remember to answer her.

"Oh, you boys must be exhausted, come on in!" She shuffles us through the door, which is almost comical, both me and D being well over six feet but she tries anyway. "It was only an hour's drive, we're not that tired." Darius sits on the large expensive sofa in the living room.

Growing up here was almost entirely lonely. My father spent most of his time buying large empty looking pieces of furniture to fill this large empty looking house. There was no comfort or feeling of family. Only a handful of family photos, most consisting of himself and Marie.

"You boys hungry? Mason, your father is still on a business call. Should be done in an hour." I turned to Marie, jaw clenched.

"He knew we were coming and couldn't take an hour off to greet us?" Bitterness runs through my veins reminding me why I rarely come home.

"He tries his best Mason." She defends him.

"Sure." I stand again, dropping my duffle to the side of the couch not bothering to bring it up to my room yet. "Darius and I are going to hit Joe's for a bit. We'll be back." Darius takes the hint and stands while awkwardly shuffling over to the door.

"See ya." I close the front door to a confused-looking Marie and instantly take a deep breath.

Leaving that house is almost as relieving as taking a piss after holding it in for hours. Painful but refreshing.

"That was something. Want to talk about it?" I kept my life as private as possible which means even my closest friends, including Darius, know very little about my home life. It took me years to get to where I am and to the point, I no longer needed to rely on my father for help.

"Not before I have at least three beers in me." I direct him to the garage where my old pickup still sits. I bought it for my eighteenth birthday with the money I had saved from working at the local gym. It wasn't much, but it was mine.

"You know you can talk to us about this shit," he gestures to my house as it gets smaller in the distance. "I know. I'm good." I assure him, not feeling like going head first into a therapeutic session on my way to the bar. I'd much prefer to get lost in the alcohol and forget it ever happened.

The town of Portsneck was as small as it was unimportant. Not much happened here besides the occasional football game that was the town's number one prized possession. I remember being in that position, playing for the high school team hoping I'd make it out to the big leagues one day just to get as far away from this place as possible. The gym I spent all my afternoons at along with any free time was less than a block from the bar, and had a parking lot that was always empty. I pull the old Ford into the closest spot to the street knowing I'll probably end up ubering home later and have to grab it in the morning.

"I can DD if you plan on having a few. Or more than a few." Darius was always observant and I fucking hated him for it. Not really but it always made me feel like I should be better at reading people.

"Thanks, man. I don't plan on getting in any trouble." He nods and follows me down the dark road.

As soon as I enter the old crowded bar I'm reminded that I'm not just Mason Jones, a local football superstar who will make it one day. No, I'm

Mason Jones who's brought his team to the Super Bowl, won it, and is on the road to doing it again. How wrong that assumption is as I'm only the smallest part of the team but when people look at me I'm convinced that's all they see. Heads turn and people whisper to their friends. I spot an open booth in the back corner and bee-line for it, ignoring the gaping stares as best as possible.

"Oh my god. Mason Jones is here." Two girls attempt a whisper but fail miserably. I flash them my signature smile accompanied by a wave. Their eyes widen and they turn to one another freaking out. Now that will never get old.

"Alright superstar. Don't let it get to your head." D claps me on the back, taking a seat. Just as I'm about to follow suit I spot a group of guys I used to hang with.

"Oh, no way. I'm going to say hi to some old friends. Grab me a beer?" Darius nods his head and I drop a twenty on the table. Tucking my wallet in the back of my dark wash jeans I walk down memory lane and catch up with my old friends. They turn their heads the second they see me and it's refreshing to have a genuine reaction to my presence and not the very common shock.

"If it isn't Mason Jones. Look at you!" It's Tony who says it, my old lifting partner from senior year of high school. I catch up with him along with the other boys around him. They tell me about their lives and what they've gotten up to in the last few years. Some of them flash wedding bands and I ignore the pang of jealousy that follows with.

"You want a beer?" Tony nudges his beer in my direction and I shake my head no. "My friend is grabbing us some." I point to the bar, turning to confirm Darius is still getting us one and not off somewhere on the phone with his wife.

My world comes to a halting stop at that moment. Sitting next to my chatty friend who is very much not on the phone, is Delilah McKenna.

My entire career was centered around control and thinking quickly under pressure. But nothing could have prepared me for seeing the girl I almost married in a red dress I remember oh so well, stumbling through the hands of my friend and out of Joe's bar.

I don't think, I just move.

Before I know it I'm outside the bar, voices, and chatter disappearing behind me. I'm focused solely on the person who's wearing far too little for a cool night like tonight.

"Delilah?" I somehow found my voice which I was sure had crawled up and left.

She stops in her tracks, red hair that was once brown cascading down her back. I squeeze my hands into fists at the sight of her.

"Holy shit, it is you." Now that she's completely turned around, I get a good enough look at the girl I loved more than anything four years ago. The girl I promised to marry.

The girl that broke my heart more than I ever let on.

"It's me." She's nervous.

I could tell by her fidgeting hands pulling at the hem of her dress. God, that dress. It hugs her like a second skin, showing off every wonderful part of her curves. My hands itch to touch for the first time in years.

"Hi, Mason." Her voice sends shockwaves down my spine and I clear my throat to distract my senses.

She's absolutely beautiful. She always was. Long hair that was brown back in the day, not covered in a ginger red. It suited her well enough with her pale complexion and freckled face. Freckles I had traced more times than I could count in the middle of the night like a love-struck fool.

"You dyed your hair," I say like a statement.

Good one Mason.

"I did." She pulls the small sweater thing closer to her body but I know it does nothing. I almost step forward and offer her my jacket as reflux but force myself to stay where I am.

"Well, I gotta run. Bye now." She turns quickly and I step forward after her. I reach for her arm, "Wait Del." As soon as I make contact with her arm I feel almost immediately the loss of her as a whole. The feeling of holding her brought me back and sent sparks down my arm. But for some reason I didn't feel weird about touching her, and I didn't want to stop.

This was all too much all at once. She turns around and looks up at me again. At this angle, I can see her blue eyes clearly and I want to pause the world at this moment to bottle it up.

"How are you?" I drop my arm reluctantly and take a step back giving her space. I wondered if she too was remembering us. It came in flashes behind every blink, like watching your own life play out in a stop motion picture film.

"I'm good. I'd ask how you are but I'd say pretty good considering your recent super bowl ring." She smiles a familiar smile and my stomach flips. "Congratulations." I've heard that same sentiment thousands of times from friends, family, and fans. None of them ever make me believe it wholeheartedly as it does coming from her mouth.

"Thank you." I instantly try and think of something else to talk about, the last time having had a full conversation with her being something I often force myself to forget. "Do you need a ride home?" I notice she's alone and that thought makes me clench angry.

She shakes her head while flashing me a lit-up iPhone. "I have an Uber on the way." Her voice trembles for a moment and it makes my heart break. We both watch as the car pulls up and she checks the license plate to confirm it's the right one.

I'm losing this moment, losing her.

Again.

"Don't go. Let's have a drink, and catch up." I throw a bone hoping she grabs it. But I see the moment her eyes dim and the soft smile on her face drops. I want to go back to seconds ago when she was nervous but content to see me.

"I'm sorry but I don't think that's a good idea. Goodbye Mason. Good luck with the season." I don't stop her as she steps forward entering the white corolla. I watch as it rolls away from the bar and away from me.

I swear out loud to no one in particular and turn around. I walk over to the wall and slam my back to the cold brick, relaxing my head back and closing my eyes.

I didn't need this right now. I didn't need my past I desperately tried to forget, coming back. But it did, and all I can think about now is how I'm not letting that woman walk away again without answers for myself and my sanity.

We were once everything to each other.

Let's hope she remembers that.

3 - Delilah

"Ok ok, breathe. I'm going to need you to breathe Del. And tell me everything."

Clara tried to calm me down on the phone, forcing me to take a minute. But it seemed almost impossible as I stripped from my red dress and paced my childhood room in nothing but my underwear.

"Mason is back. He's here." I wince at the way it sounds coming out from between my lips.

He looked so good. So fucking good. I almost forgot how tall he was but was instantly reminded when he stepped out of that bar looking like a deer caught in headlights. His dark wash jeans clung to his muscular yet lean thighs and he wore a long sleeve shirt that was begging for mercy as it stuck to his arms. Arms that had been around me at one point. Arms that I knew all too well how comforting and reassuring arms could be.

"EARTH TO DELILAH!" The scream of my friend, still on the phone, tears me away from my very detailed encounter with a certain pro football star. "I'm here," I said.

My cat, Anakin, who I named after just finishing my binge-watch of the prequels, brushed up against my bare leg, begging for attention. I scooped him up in all his brown tabby cat glory and brought him up to my bed where he remained the only man I needed.

Slipping on a large oversized shirt, an old one of my dad's, I took a seat on the edge of my bed and filled Clara in on everything.

She was quiet by the end of the conversation, her mind probably just as blank as mine right now.

"Well, did he look happy to see you? Sad? Mad?" She ponders. I think back to his reaction to finally seeing my face and it tears at my soul. It was nothing but shock and admiration, one of which he used to look at me with, day in and day out.

"He looked at me like I killed his puppy, Clara," I confess. She laughs at my obvious over-exaggeration. "I highly doubt it. I bet he just looked at you like his ex-girlfriend showed up at the same bar as him. Oh wait...that's exactly what happened." Her sarcastic reply had me rolling my eyes.

"Very funny. But seriously, I think I'm going to need some serious girls' nights for the next few weeks to recover from that." There is nothing more that I want than to forget that what just happened, did happen.

It doesn't stop me from pulling up Instagram and typing Mason Jones in the search bar. Neither does it stop me from cursing myself as I lay eyes on his profile.

I still see hints of the boy I fell in love with all those years ago, but they're stuffed in with everything that makes him the man he is now. In most of his pictures he looks sad or moody, never really smiling. He's got plenty of posts up with his teammates and even more with that friend from the bar, Darius I realize, from a tagged photo. He's built the life he always wished to live. I find myself smiling, a sad smile knowing he did it all like he said he would, just not together.

"Listen, Del, people fall apart. What you guys had was epic. But you were both young and foolishly in love. Don't beat yourself up over the past, okay?" Clara has always been my voice of reason and I love her for that.

"You're right." I exit the app, leaving the follow button blue and not hitting follow back.

I remember the day I unfollowed him from everything like it was yesterday. We agreed to keep it civil and even still be friends, but it got harder to pretend to myself. Seeing him out in other cities with new friends and new girls was just too hard to bear.

"I'm always right. Now let me get my shit together and let Ryan know I'm ditching her for you." Clara and Ryan had been living together now for almost a year and had been together even longer. They both met during their senior year of university at a Jazz show that they both needed to go to for class credit. Neither of them knew a thing about Jazz or each other but by the end of the night, they were already halfway in love as Clara says.

"Okay, see you soon." I hang up, scoop Anakin into my arms and forget all about my past, a six-foot quarterback that was once mine, and close my eyes while I wait for my best friend to come over.

~ ~ ~

"Can I have one order of your hashbrowns and an iced oat milk latte please?" I rattle off my morning order while fixing my hair up in a ponytail. The ends were dry and cracked, a reminder I needed a haircut along with a touch-up.

I decided to dye my hair red when I got into PA school as congratulations to myself considering I had always wanted to do it.

"Here you go, miss." I thank the barista and leave a tip in the jar.

I step aside from the crowd that's gathered at the end of the coffee bar. Scanning the small cafe I find a spot in the front windows with a small table and two chairs. Deciding that this is where I'm going to spend my Sunday studying. My notes were something I put all my energy into whenever I could, I figured out the only way to succeed in my classes was by studying: shocker.

After my night with Clara and Ryan, who also came over because she heard who I ran into, I decided that I needed today to do something I knew. Even though I planned to take the day off, studying and planning was the one thing in life I had complete control of so I settled on that.

I made sure to leave Anakin at home with lots of hidden treats around the house and plenty of water.

I barely get the opportunity to open up my laptop because the second I reach for my bag I spot a familiar figure walking across the street. He wears black sweatpants that hang low on his hips and I catch a sliver of skin between that and his tight compression long-sleeve shirt, also black.

It seems like fate has another plan for me this weekend.

First, the douchebag who decided he couldn't dignify me with remembering my name. And now, my past decided to crash right into me in full force wearing that boyish smile I fell In love with as a young teen.

I almost packed up my barely settled self but then I stopped myself. I didn't do anything wrong, none of us did. I could get through the awkward exchanges with an ex just like everyone else in the world does, I don't need to hide away like a coward no matter how hard I want to.

So that's why when he walks through the door and scans the open store I don't hide away the moment his eyes find mine. He does a double-take for a short second and then takes a few short strides over to my secluded table. I should've sat in the back away from everyone else to avoid wandering eyes. If his height wasn't enough to grab attention his fame status just might.

"Hi."

His hair is messy and lined with a thin line of sweat. From his disheveled appearance and flushed face, I can only assume he had just come from the gym. I force myself not to take a quick look at his large chest which I'm sure has only benefited from his years in the gym. Instead, I lift my head and meet his expecting gaze.

"Hello." I smile.

He looks lost for a second as if debating what to say next.

"Can I sit for a moment?" He points to the empty chair across from me and I internally curse the lack of friends I have at the moment that could be filling that spot.

"Sure." I distract myself by taking a sip of my cold latte. He reaches a hand down to the small chair which looks ridiculous in comparison to his large palm. He pulls it from the table and takes a seat, knees brushing my own under below.

Shit.

I sat back, ignoring the way the single brush of his legs had me clenching my own.

"How was your night?" He looks awkward and completely out of place. Something I doubt happens often.

"Pretty good, yours?" I ask.

"It was alright." He shifts forward resting his strong forearms on the white top. He clasps his hands in a closed grip together just inches from my coffee, close enough for the condensation to drip onto his finger.

"You look great Del." He speaks again, eyes tracing my frizzy hair that I should've dignified with another brush this morning. I'm wearing no makeup at all and my glasses are two years old because I couldn't find my usual ones. I can only imagine how I look sitting across from a literal professional athlete.

"Thank you, and so do you," I replied.

We stare at one another for a moment too long to be just strangers.

"What brings you to town?" We talk like we've never met.

It fucking hurts.

"Season starts next week. Came home to visit Dad and Marie." He reaches for the straw wrapper that sits on the table and starts to rip it slowly. "Oh, that's good." God, I sound like a teacher trying to get to know her student. Formal and cordial, I hate it.

"What about you? I thought you were staying in Penn for PA school?" His brows furrow and he turns his attention from the wrapper back to me. I pinch my leg where my hands are clasped to ignore the clench of my heart.

"I had to come home." That is all I say. Not wanting to go into detail about the last four years of my life with him.

He nods his head, leaning back about to say something else but before he gets the chance I interrupt. "We don't have to do this. The whole catching up on each other's lives thing." I gesture between us hoping he agrees.

"Don't do that." He drops the wrapper and leans forward again. Eyes darkening and face hardening. "It's been years Delilah, don't act like I don't care to know what's happened in your life." I don't breathe for a solid three seconds before answering.

"You've been busy." He shakes his head at my response.

"I was never too busy for you Delilah. You-" he points to me. "Decided that all on your own." Oh, we're not doing this.

I shake my head and lean completely back in my chair. I'm not doing this again, we're not doing this again. I'm going to pack my stuff and get the hell out of here before I have the same useless conversation again. I don't think my heart can take more of the back and forth that was our relationship.

"I'm not doing this again." I stand abruptly but so does he. "Sit down Delilah. I'm not leaving this cafe until we talk." He crosses his arms like he has full control over me and this situation.

"We did talk, Mason. Four years ago." I imagine we look like those old cowboy films doing a standoff in the middle of Fuel Rush cafe.

He clenches his jaw and it momentarily distracts me. I wish he wasn't so goddamn beautiful, maybe then I'd have better luck at staying mad at him. But I'm not mad. I'm over it, I've been over this and him for years now. At least that's what I'm telling myself every time a memory I so forcefully shove down, reaches the surface.

"Delilah. Please." He begs. "I'm not leaving like this. Not again. I'm not asking you for anything more than to just talk." I watch as he steps forward around the stupid table that should be larger to make him walk longer. When he's just a breath away I close my eyes but it does nothing to stop the alarming realization that he smells the same as he did before.

Everything about it invades my senses and I'm dizzy. This is all too much too fast. It doesn't help that he looks at me with those begging eyes. Ones that have won him more than enough points in different arguments.

"What's to talk about? You're leaving in I can only assume two days. What is the point, Mason?" I reason, begging him to see I'm doing what's best for the both of us—again.

"The point is that I've fucking missed you, Delilah. And seeing you last night was the first time in a long time that I felt like I could fucking breathe again." His hands reach for my arms but then he stops them before they reach my skin.

"I care about you. I always have." His words almost make my eyes water with tears but the reality is that I'm not the same person I was all those years ago.

"Fine." I step out of his reach, not missing the way his arms drop and hands tighten into fists. "We can catch up, but not now. I have to study." I look away from his suffocating gaze, finding the etchings on the outside wooden post more interesting at this moment.

"Dinner. I'll pick you up for dinner." He reaches into his back pocket bringing my attention back to him.

"You blocked me, um, after everything. What's your new number?" Now I'm embarrassed at him realizing I removed him from my life. But I never would've moved on if I didn't. My cheeks heat up as he passes me the phone and I type in my new number putting my name in as Delilah.

When handing it back to him his fingers brush mine and we both look at one another. He grips his phone pulling it close to him. I watch as he inspects the new contact and then to my surprise and my hearts' demise— changes my name to Del.

The nickname he started for me.

"Okay. I'll text you." He looks into my eyes for confirmation and I reluctantly nod my head in agreement. The second he leaves I take a very-needed deep breath and plop back into the cold seat.

I'm going to have a heart attack by the time whatever this is, is over.

4 - Delilah

A/N quick note — make sure you guys are reading the chapters in order !! I don't want you to miss out on any key parts!! Okay now enjoy...

~~~

"You're fucking crazy Del."

Carla rushes around my room, shuffling through all the clothes I've discarded on the floor in preparation for my, not a date— date, tonight. "I know that, thank you very much." She was right.

The second I got home from the cafe I called Carla again who almost had a heart attack at my rash decision to see Mason again later.

"I don't think this is a good idea. I mean what do you expect to get out of it? He's just going to leave again and break your heart all over." Thank you, Carla. That very important piece of information I am already well aware of and trying my best to ignore.

"I tried to tell him we didn't have to do the whole catching up thing. He was very persistent." I shove my feet through a black dress I bought for a class function two years ago. Thank god it was the stretch spandex material or else it wouldn't have survived the trip up my wide hips and lower stomach. "Turn around," her cold hands touch my back zipping the dress up.

Everything is telling me not to go tonight, knowing how hard I broke after this man. Knowing that he's my big-shot quarterback and I'm still working on the first and only goal of my adult life. The only result from this dinner would one hundred percent be another goodbye, and I've had far too many of those. I'm done saying goodbye.

"Whatever you do, do not let that man kiss you. Especially fuck you, Del. I swear if you come home telling me that I will personally drive to your house and shove a lamp up your ass." Clara always had a way with words. I laugh at her crazy insinuation for tonight.

"I'm serious. It will only make it harder." Her blonde hair is a frazzled mess on the top of her head and her eyes look dead serious.

She scares me a bit.

"I am not fucking Mason Jones. I am meeting him to get him out of this town as soon as possible so I can go back to pretending everything is okay and I don't hate my life every second of every day." I huff and sit on the end of my bed, out of breath from my rant, and suck it in to get the zipper up my back.

"I'm just as wary of this as you are, okay? I'm already feeling anxious about this, I just need you to know I'm not doing this for any other reason than to get him to leave." Clara takes a seat beside me and circles her arm behind my back. She rests her head on my shoulder and I rest mine on the top of hers.

"I know, I just don't want to see him hurt you again. You deserve more than what you've been dealt Del, I just want you to see that." I was more appreciative of my best friend than she could ever know. She was here picking up the pieces of my first and only heartbreak. She was also by my side during the worst day of my life.

I wouldn't be here without her.

"I love you. I know you're just looking out for me and I appreciate that more than you know. I'm going to get through this night and be done with it. He'll go back to forgetting I exist and I'll go back to studying my ass off." I hug my friend close, taking comfort in her presence.

We both startle at the sound of the doorbell and my heart drops.

He's here.

"Okay. Call me or text me for anything, and I mean anything! If it is going awful and you are going to break— CALL ME." Clara shakes my shoulders and I nod my head.

She rushes to the front door to let him in and I take the millisecond I have to take a deep breath and calm my racing heart. I'm going to get through this and It's going to be fine. Even if it's hard to look at him in the face without breaking inside, I'm going to get through this.

"She's just finishing up." I hear Clara say from the living room. Fuck, okay.

I rush to finish getting ready by grabbing the heels I laid out beside my bed to wear for the night along with locating my purse and coat. Once everything was in my possession and all accounted for, I stepped out of the comfort of my bedroom door and walked my way to the front of the house.

The first thing I notice is I did not mentally prepare myself to see Mason Jones in a suit. He wore all-black dress pants, a jacket, and an undershirt. He even had an untied tie hanging loosely around his neck. I forgot how to breathe while scanning the way his muscular thighs hugged his most definitely tailored pants along with how he made my average-looking living room look exceptionally tiny.

His attention snapped to me the second my heels hit the hardwood of the hallway. We made eye contact, brown on blue, and I would have paid millions to know what was going through his head at that moment.

Because the only thing going through mine is how much I had missed in the last four years. How the way he smiled looked the same but wore a different sadness these days and how his arms looked at least two times bigger than they did at twenty-one. How the person standing before me was a man and the one I fell in love with was a shell of this.

"Have her back by ten." Clara interrupts my thoughts with a pointed finger and Mason is forced to turn his attention to her command. "Okay, Clara." He smiles a bit as if finding her protectiveness amusing. We had all been friends back then, I'm sure it was just as weird seeing one another as it was for Mason and me.

"Ready?" He opens his arm for me to slip my own through but I ignore it, not needing the consequences of touching him. I step out in front of him while casting Clara a knowing glance and making my way to the truck parked out front.

"Your parents here? I'd love to say hi?" Shit. I should've thought this through.

Clara looks at me on the edge of the porch, expression nervous. Mason takes a moment looking between us two trying to read our faces before he gives up. "My dad isn't here right now. Ready?" I turn, not allowing him to dig further.

He catches up to me quickly, only taking a few steps with those long legs, and the second he does he stretches his arm forward preventing me from opening the door. "You said just your Dad, where's your mom?"

I wish he wouldn't have asked that, but if we're ripping all the band-aids off tonight, might as well answer.

"She died. Three years ago." I choke on the last word and turn away. I don't want to see any sort of pity in his eyes. I know he'd most likely feel bad for not being here but I don't want to confront that right now. We were different people living different lives.

"Shit Del. What the fuck?" He raises his arms above his head and then slowly brings them over his painfully heartbroken face. "Why the hell didn't you tell me? I had no idea." He whispers the last part and forces me to look at him with his questioning eyes.

"It was years ago. It happened so fast, I didn't handle it well." I turn back to the passenger door. "Can we get going? I have to be up early." I ignore his pleading face, not wanting to talk a single breath more about my mother tonight. There was only so much I could rightfully handle.

"Fine. But we are talking about this." He walks off mumbling something to himself and I almost feel bad for not reaching out all those years ago. But I was grieving and he was—well he was on top of the world. He didn't need an ex-girlfriend weighing him down with sad news just as he had gotten his starting position on a beloved football team.

I take my seat, close the door, and am once again transported back into memories I wished to not repeat. He drove the same old beat-up Ford as he did in college and something about that sentiment made me smile. It was still him no matter how different we were now.

"How about that Italian place? It's new right?" He types something into his phone before turning it off and focusing on me. All of a sudden I am hyper-aware of how small the space of this cabin is and how close he is. I can smell his cologne and see the small lines on his face.

"Sounds good." I smile hoping it doesn't look forced. Why not go back to the same place I was left at dinner with an ex who I'm pretty sure will turn every head the second we step through the door? What could go wrong?

5 - Mason

I called plays for a living. I surveyed a situation, made a decision, and made it happen within the snap of a second. I was used to being under pressure, or at least I should've been.

I was completely thrown off my game here. Sitting in my passenger seat is someone I thought I'd never get the opportunity of having a conversation with again. Someone I have no right looking at the way I do whenever we stop at a red light.

"I'll park down on Wick street, you don't mind walking?" I take a quick look to my right at the woman beside me. She's wearing a regular black dress but makes it look like a runway piece. Everything about her is show-stopping and jaw-dropping. When she came around the corner from her room I would've believed someone if they told me my heart stopped because that's what it felt like. Seeing her there for the first time in... years. Last night was just a tease, just a glimpse into the years I've missed but today. Today was a full fucking semi-truck reminder.

"That's fine." Her face is turned so I can't read her.

I know she didn't want to come out tonight and maybe she was right. But I wasn't just going to show up and leave again without having a conversation. And then the news about her mom? I mean fuck. I would've dropped everything to be there for her and she knows that. So much has changed in the last four years and it makes me go crazy.

I drove in complete silence, none of us knowing what to say to one another. I wanted her to talk to me, tell me everything about what happened in the time we've been apart. I still craved to know her in the deepest ways possible and I hated myself for that. We were broken up, she broke it off. I shouldn't crave these things.

I park my truck in an open spot just a block away and make sure to make it around to her side before she could open the door to help her down.

She looked surprised when I offered her my hand to help her out, but she took it nonetheless. It was a double-edged sword. The feeling of her skin on mine sent me into a cold sweat, gone was the common feeling of revolution and in its place was familiarity. As if my body knew hers like it was it's own.

Fuck.

"I'm glad to see you opted for a coat tonight." Her jacket last night was a poor excuse for a cover-up. It left little to the imagination and did nothing against the frigid air. I hated the idea that she was freezing, it left me uncomfortable.

"Yes, I learn from my mistakes." I stilled at her words, sensing a double meaning.

"Good." Not knowing what else to say I rested my hand on the small of her back, directing us both into the restaurant and to a table, I had already reserved. The chatter seemed to die down a tone and I ignored it the best I could. If I could make it through the night without interruption it would be a miracle.

I want her to feel comfortable talking to me, not freaked out because people keep staring and snapping pictures of my every move.

"Thank you," she says while sliding down into the chair I've pulled out for her. I watch as she sheds the jacket and holds my breath at the sight of her bare shoulders. I'm a fucking goner.

"Have you been here before?" I ask.

This is a newer restaurant in town and a bit pricey. Money was never the issue in my family but I hadn't been home enough to explore the new spots to eat. Nor would I want to because it'd mean I'd be doing it with my father.

"Yes, unfortunately." The last part was a whisper and I watched her lips curl into a smirk and cheeks flush red. "Unfortunately?" I pray. She was always so open and talkative when I knew her. Everyone knew Delilah and her kind soul. She'd talk to anyone about anything to make sure they felt comfortable or seen. It was one of the qualities I fell in love with. So this awkward silence and double-meaning short answers are killing me.

"Bad date."

Of course, she's been dating, of course, she has. I wouldn't expect her not to be. But hearing it come from her lips doesn't make it hurt any less.

"Oh. Do I even want to know?" She laughs at my reply and it takes a weight off my shoulders. "No, I don't think you do." Her smile is the greatest gift and I feel like one lucky bastard to see it tonight.

"I'm sorry about your mom Del. I would've been here." I'm still not over the little fact she felt as though she couldn't tell me her goddamn mother died. Rosie was the sweetest person on this earth and a huge part of Delilah's life, I would've dropped everything. I think I still would.

"I was going through a lot at the time. I barely spoke to anyone. You had better things like starting your career, I wouldn't expect you to come to that." She's crazy. That's the only logical explanation for how insane she sounds right now. After we broke up she must've gone crazy.

"Don't make it sound like a burden. That was your mother for god's sake! I would've been here for you." I shift forward already feeling myself getting angry. "You know that. I told you that." My voice is almost a whisper, not wanting to turn heads.

She looks away from me and I almost reach over to bring her eyes back to me, but instead, I sit back and clear my throat.

What the fuck happened between us? What gave her the impression that I wouldn't be here? I just want us to be able to talk like we used to, even before we were dating, we were friends. We could talk about whatever is on our minds without expectations. I want that from her tonight. I think we both need it.

"You're right, I should've told you. But that's in the past. I'm not sitting here all night discussing what went wrong. We're not doing that." What she was saying made sense and I knew I should agree. I couldn't help the feeling of wanting more no matter how hard I tried to bury it. That's what it was always like between us. Always.

"Fine. Just know, that is not the case. You're not a burden and nothing would've been more important than seeing you when you needed it." As soon as I said it I knew it was too much. Too much all at once.

We're strangers now. Our lives are no longer with each other. I don't get to tell her things like that and make it harder on us both.

"Sorry, just. You know what I mean." I distract myself from the lame attempt at not looking like a crazy ex and pick up my menu. Before I find the entree options I catch a glimpse of her face that's wearing a crazy blush and a small smile.

"How is your father?" She asks after a while.

We put our food order in and got our drinks. She settles on the house white wine and myself on a beer. Not much has changed on that end.

"He's good." I'd rather not talk about my father tonight. "And yours?" I switched the conversation back to her.

"He's good." She clears her throat. "It's been hard. He uh, as expected, is having a hard time with mom's passing even now. But he's doing his best." She looks down at her hands that are crossed on the table.

"I can only imagine." I accepted my plate of food as the waitress set it down in front of us. She smiles at me and then at Delilah. For a second I wonder if they know one another due to Delilah's knowing smile and recognition across the waitress' face.

We eat in silence for the majority of the time. Both of us not knowing what to say to one another. She takes every awkward silence as an opportunity to continue eating or taking a bite of her pasta dish.

Maybe this was a bad idea. Maybe I should've just said hi and been done with it. I'm leaving in a day, this can't possibly be anything more than a dinner and catching up. So why did I put us through this? Make it awkward?

"So earlier you mentioned you couldn't finish PA school. What for?"

She drops her fork and looks up at me with a sad look on her face.

"Uhm, not yet. After mom died I went home and took some time off. I didn't have the opportunity to continue after graduation." Fuck.

While I was getting drafted and moving to an entirely new state she was over here having the worst years of her life. All she talked about when we were together was going to school and becoming a PA. It was her biggest goal in life and she was one hell of a student. Always studying late at night, and staying after classes to speak to professors. I can't imagine how hard it was for her to drop it all.

Tonight was a bad idea. I feel like complete shit. Everything that comes out of her mouth is just a reminder of what I fucked up.

"Delilah," I sigh and lean my head in my hands. "You're killing me." I wish we were alone. I don't care if we're strangers or it's awkward between us because at this moment I'd crush her to my chest in a hug we both need.

I need it.

"I'm so fucking sorry. I know how much you wanted to go to school. I can't imagine how hard it was to drop it. Are you almost done now?" She watches my mouth as I talk and grips her hands tighter.

She comes off strong and unaffected but I know better. I know better than anyone in this room that the girl across from me is hurting. Seeing me again is hurting her. Maybe it's the reminder of what we lost together or maybe it's a reminder of her life before all the bad shit she was dealt.

But I was the cause of it all right now.

"It's okay. And yea, I graduate this year. I'm doing my clinical here in Portsneck to be closer to dad if he needs me." It all made sense. She had probably gone back to Pennsylvania for the program she had wanted years after she planned.

"Well, that's good. I'm proud of you." I was. I truly was. If anyone deserved anything on this planet it was most definitely Delilah McKenna.

"Thank you, Mason." She smiles a smile that resembles sunlight. It's bright and warm, just like she is.

She tells me about her friends she met along the way along with how her clinic is going. It's going well and she's liking the specialty she's in. My chest fills with pride as I hear her talk about her passions and dreams finally coming true.

"The check." The waitress from before sets the thin white sheet of paper between us and looks at Delilah. "Make sure he at least pays half." She winks and Delilah laughs and I'm left confused.

"What is that supposed to mean?" They both look at me with knowing glances. The waitress just shakes her head and leaves. I watch as Delilah attempts to grab the check in the middle of the table but before she has the opportunity I beat her to it.

"Don't even try it." I stare her down watching her roll her eyes. "What did the waitress mean?" I reach for my wallet in my back pocket, to grab my card. Once out, I place it on the table with the check.

"Let's just say I had to pay for a date and dinner due to his need to leave." She blushes like she's embarrassed and my blood boils.

"You're telling me you were left here?" That's all I hear from that.

"Yes." She looks away.

"Delilah. You deserve better than that." The waitress grabs the check, notices it's my card, and winks at Delilah across the table.

"I know." She settles back in her chair, finishing off her glass of wine. "Thank you for that but I could've split it." She eyes the card that's now back in my hands. I tip the waitress and pack up my wallet.

"Not a chase Del." I wink for good measure which causes another deep blush to form on her cheeks. She's too easy.

"Ready?" I stand, making sure I've got everything on me before going around the table to help her up. She stands slowly and her arm brushes against my chest while she turns around. I focus on anything but that for my sanity.

We make our way out of the restaurant and just as I'm about to ask her another question the door opens up and two men step out.

"Dude, I'm sorry to do this. We figured we'd wait until you were done with your date or whatever but, can we get an autograph?" I watch Delilah still next to me.

"Oh, sure thing." At least they had the decency to wait. Most would interrupt.

I sign their phones with a sharpie they pulled from their pocket. They thanked me and apologized again before stepping back into the restaurant.

"You're so... famous." My attention snaps back to Delilah who leans against the brick wall by the door, watching.

"Not really." I step towards her.

She tenses when I reach where she stands against the wall. I watch the rise and fall of her chest, and hear the small short breaths she takes as if smelling my cologne. The one I wore tonight was one she always loved. I never stopped wearing it.

"Yes really." She smiles up at me.

I step forward again, praying she doesn't push me back.

She doesn't.

She inhales when I bring my arms to her sides, caging her in. Lowering my head to her neck, I'm careful not to touch her skin.

"I've missed you."

She pauses, eyes closing.

"I missed you too."

6 - Delilah

He was so close, I could feel his breath.

Memories of mornings together laying in bed just the two of us, wrapped up in one another infiltrated my mind. The familiarity of it overwhelmed every single one of my senses. Like the feeling of the morning light while wrapped up in bed, comfortable and warm.

Even after all these years he still had the same effect on both my body and mind. He's close enough that we can breathe the same air. His nearness is a reminder of how this was second nature before It was forgotten.

I watch him lean down even closer. If moved even in the slightest our lips would brush one another's in a kiss. I couldn't breathe. My heart was racing a mile a minute and my hands flexed and unflexed beside him as if needing something to grab that wasn't him. I needed to remain level-headed.

He was breathing real heavy, his chest moving up and down erratically like the pace of my own heart. His eyes were closed but mine were wide open now wanting to remember this moment and paint a picture of my past.

He moves his body closer, almost touching my own, and goes in to press his lips to my mine, but before he gets the opportunity I turn my head at the last minute, and his soft but cool lips land on my skin. I am still at the contact, completely aware of the way his lips feel against me.

"Mason." He stills, pulling back. I hear him swear under his breath and I almost reach out to squeeze his arm.

He knows we shouldn't be doing this. We shouldn't be pretending like there isn't a reason we broke up and left one another all those years ago. We are back in the same position but this time it's a weekend. Just forty-eight hours of confusion and remembering what was lost. Even less time to make sense of it all.

"Del," he sighs and steps back just a step, all while keeping his eyes trained on my face. His gaze was like a tattoo gun, leaving traces of invisible ink along my skin and the heat of it all in its wake.

His eyes were pained and his jaw clenched like he wanted to say more. Say anything. But I know he knows we can't do this again, and like last time I was the one who stepped up and did it for us. I'd do that again if I had to, at this moment. He has a heart of gold and always struggles to say what we both knew, so I do it for him

"We both know how this ends." I smile up at him, wanting to remember the good and not the bad. "You're going back up to Boston tomorrow. Don't make this hard."

He nods his head, dropping both arms from around me. I don't miss the way his hands clench into fists as if grasping for what could have been.

"I hate how reasonable you are sometimes." His voice is a whisper almost lost in the night wind but I catch it anyway. It's suddenly a whole lot cooler standing against this wall without his body heat surrounding me.

"Someone has to be."

"I know." He sighs and turns to the street.

Maybe if times were different. Maybe if he didn't have to leave again and I didn't have to finish off school, then just maybe things could end differently. I might've let him kiss me tonight under the stars in our old hometown like we were teenagers again. I might've even let him come home with me.

Maybe.

But not in this reality.

"I'll take you home then. Don't want Clara killing me." He tries to joke. Tries to lighten the already heavy air between us. As if a joke could be a bandaid on the already fractured night.

"Okay."

Walking back to the car is almost entirely silent. There aren't many people out and about on the sidewalk but the few that do a double take at who walks next to me. They stop and gasp but then keep going as if remembering he's a real person and it's rude to stare.

I don't blame them.

By the time we make it to his truck, I'm all out of ideas on what to talk about. I no longer feel the need to fill the silence between us with pointless conversations that go nowhere. He's leaving tomorrow to go back to the real world and I stay here.

There is no new possibility for us. There never was. This was just supposed to be catching up.

"Here." Before he starts the truck he hands me a piece of paper. "Don't open it right now. But it's something I had meant to give you a long time ago."

Oh god.

Did he write me a letter?

I look over at him. He's already looking at me with the same sad eyes as before. I look down at the notepaper in his hand and take it from him. The paper is almost weightless but it feels like a steel bar as I shove it into my purse.

"Okay," I nod my head. I try not to think too much about what's written on that paper because If I did I might go crazy. I'd save whatever it was for a time I needed it most. Now I needed this moment more than anything.

We drive in silence and I begin to appreciate the idea of living in a small town because it's only a short drive back to my house. The entire time I spend it looking out my window, knowing if I were to take any glances to my left I'd just be pained with what I saw.

We reached my house almost an hour before ten o'clock. Something I'm sure Clara would be happy about. Something I should be happy about but I can't shake the feeling of forcing another goodbye. I knew going into this night that nothing could come from it and therefore should be grateful I'm home early. But I felt the complete opposite.

"Delilah." He pulls my attention from my hands and I'm staring holes in my lap. "I'm going to walk you to the door, is that alright?" I nod my head, unable to form any words.

Why did I hurt so easily? Why did I love so easily?

He opens my door and holds out his hand for me to take. I step down, placing my palm into his, giving myself this last bit of comfort. He walks me to the door like he said he would and with each step I feel as though I'm back in that apartment building walking down the hall as he stands in the bedroom in tears.

We both stop once I reach the door. I turn to look at him and force a smile.

"Thank you, Mason. It was good to see you." I wish he'd just smile as he used to one more time for me. But that wasn't the case. He looked angry and sad all in one. His eyebrows were furrowed and lips set in a grim line.

He also never dropped my hand.

His head tilts down to look at our interlocked palms as if taking a mental picture like I just was about his smile. I wonder if he's thinking the same as me. I wonder if he can't wait to leave to go back to his bachelor life in the city and forget about me and this weekend.

"You too, Del." He finally looks up at me, and this time with a soft smile. His finger traces the back of my hand in soft strokes and he takes a step forward. I hold my breath as he leans down to press his soft lips to my forehead.

I close my eyes, breathing him in one last time.

When he pulls back his face is hardened like he's getting ready for a game.

"Just give me this. Call me. I need you to call me this time. For anything, okay? If you want to just talk about your shitty day or if something terrible happens as it did to your mom, you call me Delilah?" His tone is serious and it has me straightening my back.

I don't feel like explaining to him that If I call him, if I keep a connection I will feed on that hope. My mind and soul will grasp it. I can't go down that road again.

"Okay," I say. He looks at me like he knows I'm lying but nods anyway.

He steps back taking one last glance at my face before turning around and walking back to his truck. He doesn't take another look back and at that moment I know I'm not alone in what I'm feeling. I know that he's feeling it too and for some reason, I find comfort in that toxic feeling of something we both know we once had but can't have again.

I watch as he pulls away from the curb, leaving behind nothing but that notepaper in my purse and a trail of exhaust.

I tell myself the same thing I told myself four years ago.

It's going to be okay.

We're both going to be okay.

7 - Delilah

Two Months Later

Holidays weren't the same anymore without her.

Nothing was the same without her. My mom was my rock, my light, and everything to me. My mother was my best friend and the holidays were a reminder of the loss in my life without her around anymore. Death was weird. It is strange and sometimes unfathomable.

One moment a person is here on this earth making cherishable memories with you and the next they are gone.

Completely.

Even as I set the table in her hand-knit Christmas-themed table runner, I felt the loss four years later. As I decorated the tree with ornaments that were once her mother's and now mine. As I laid out the cookies and milk, not forgetting the carrots for the reindeer.

It was all a reminder of what I once had.

Dad was in the living room watching It's A Wonderful Life. Another tradition painted in all things mom. He was quiet as always, resting his head on the palm of his hand just sitting there silently. He struggled with the loss of mom even all these years later.

At first, I was afraid I was going to lose him too, which is what led me to do my clinical year here in Portsneck and to live at home with him throughout the.

"Dad, it's ready."

I set the stuffing next to the turkey, my favorite combination.

It was still light out as we were having an early Christmas Eve dinner. I had to work tonight in the hospital emergency room. Something I started doing as my interest in the PA program at school. I needed to work Christmas Eve so that I could have Christmas day off and spend it with Dad, Clara, and her family.

A new tradition started after mom.

"It looks amazing honey. Thank you." I feel the brush of my dad's gray beard as he kisses my forehead before taking a seat at the head of the table.

"Stuffing made just how you like it." I pass him the bowl, taking a seat to his left. "And the gravy was made just how grandma used to make it." I pointed to the gravy boat. He smiles down at his plate and I swallowed a bite of turkey ignoring the tension.

Dinners were hard without the pressure of a Holiday. My father didn't have a good relationship with his parents so they never came around for the holidays. I made an effort to call them once in a while, knowing it was what mom would've wanted me to continue doing. She was always the one encouraging my father to mend the relationship to no avail.

"Amazing," he chewed a piece of turkey and gave me a thumbs up.

We ate in silence, listening to the faint sound of It's A Wonderful Life playing in the background. We passed one another more stuffing and gravy, both of our favorites until there was almost nothing left. I buy the smallest turkey I can and make just the right amount of stuffing and mashed potatoes, after years of practicing our favorite comfort meal. The leftovers are amazing, but I know we will have a ton tomorrow.

"You have work tonight?" Dad breaks the silence, taking a bite of his apple pie.

Store-bought because my baking skills are nonexistent.

"Yes, overnight. I'll be back in the morning just in time to open presents from Santa." I joke, trying to get him to laugh.

My mother still helped me set out the milk and cookies even well into my teen years, and even up until she died. It was something we always did to keep the tradition of holiday spirit, a way of connecting to our childhood together.

It was my favorite.

"You know he's not real. I can't believe you still do that." I swallow, reaching for my glass. His tone shifted to something darker and I immediately want to fix it. "I know that Dad. But as you know, Mom and I–" he cut me off.

"Mom's not here anymore." His fist slams down on the table and I feel the tug of grief in my chest. "We need to move on. We need to stop pretending everything is okay. We need, we need—." He huffs out, standing up and walking away from the table wiping his eyes.

I stare at the empty table and the half-eaten apple pie.

I try not to cry but I can't stop the cool tears from leaking and I make no move to wipe them away. This is how it always went with any mention of my mom. It's like he wanted me to completely erase her for his convenience. As if it wasn't hard enough for me, but for him, I couldn't talk about it.

I shoved my hands over my face and sobbed.

I sobbed for the time lost with my mom due to cancer. I sobbed for my father's broken heart and I sobbed for my own heart. Once full of love, now full of dread and guilt.

~~~

I sat in my room now, doing my hair and makeup before work. It was almost seven and my shift started at eight pm, the hospital was only a short drive away.

I had cleaned up the table after Dad left it, storing away the apple pie for him later and ignoring the way it was another failed family dinner between the two of us. He would do this often, get mad at a mention of mom and take it out on me, then feel bad afterward. It was a cycle, an endless one that forced him into therapy.

Therapy that I prayed would help eventually.

Carefully opening my door to not wake or disturb him, I sped walk through the house and out the door avoiding any conversation that could happen. I was about to have a twelve-hour shift and after the day I had, I didn't need another argument on top of the weight of the conversation earlier.

Starting my car I pulled my black winter jacket closer to my body, tucked my chin, and waited for the car to warm up. A downfall of living in New England is the harsh winter season. No matter how many years I've lived here I'd never get over the cold, or get used to it.

Pulling out my phone I open my messages to see two unread texts. One was from my friend Tish from school asking if I wanted to study with her this weekend. I reply yes to her and slowly hover over the other unread message.

Mason: This is me keeping my promise and staying in touch. Hope you're well.

He sent it one week ago. A whole week staring at it wondering if I should reply or not. A full week of Clara just telling me to delete it and let it go. I wish I could, I wish. But every time I found myself sliding my finger over the message to delete I just couldn't.

So I leave it there, taunting me.

Shoving my phone into my bag I put my seatbelt on, reverse and make the short drive to work. The roads in the wintertime were always the worst around here, and I hated driving on them. Not to mention the potholes that are created due to the snowplows, absolutely awful.

As soon as I pull into my spot I get an incoming call from Clara who from what I know should be mid-Christmas Eve dinner with her parents. They always spent both days together, waking up the next morning and opening presents, just like I once did.

I answer her call through the Bluetooth connection in my car, only having a few minutes.

"Hello?"

I should've known something was up the second she called. She never called so close to my work time not to mention during her family dinner. I should've known that it was already a shitty holiday so why not make it worse?

I should've known.

"Delilah. Where are you?" Her voice is full of concern and my heart rate picks up.

"In my car, at work. Why?" I rush. "You're scaring me, what happened?"

I immediately think of all the awful possibilities of why she is calling me concerned on Christmas Eve, none of them making me feel any better about this phone call.

"It's Mason." She pauses. "He's hurt. Real bad Del. We were watching the game and it happened so fast. They rushed him off the field." She takes a deep breath.

My heart stops at that moment.

I usually always watched Mason's games in secret or kept tabs on him and the score when I could. I was always watching, because of this fear. He had gotten minor injuries when we were together. Sprains, bruises, and minor concussions.

Nothing that would warrant Clara saying, it's bad.

It's bad.

"What," I found my voice. "How bad, what are the reporters saying?" I pick at my nail bed, my heart rate not slowing down. I take a deep breath.

"I don't know babe. They just said something about his shoulder. It was after a bad sack. Looks like he landed on it. I just thought you should have heard it from me before you saw it." Oh god.

"Fuck," is all I say.

"I know. After seeing him again for the first time in a while and now this? I'm sorry Del." I can hear her family talking in the background in hushed voices.

"It's okay. Thank's for telling me. I'll call you tomorrow, I have to go to work." A lie, I have ten minutes, but I need all ten to relax. She says okay and tells me to call her if I need her before I hang up.

Mason is hurt. Potentially really bad. My ex-boyfriend who I saw for the first time in years, two months ago, is hurt. And I couldn't even answer his text. Shame instantly washes over me. I feel awful.

I pull up the game footage and feel sick to my stomach watching him get sacked. The defensemen came through the pocket, right to him. His arm was up ready to throw when the defensive end took him down. I watch his face screw up into pain and listen to the announcers go quiet. I turned it off.

Oh my god.

There is no news on his exact injury, only a report of him being rushed to the nearby hospital. It has to be his shoulder, as it's what he landed on. His throwing shoulder. I tell myself that he's in the NFL and that he will be treated with a high priority in his care, but it does nothing to settle my nerves.

After all these years of radio silence and him playing at his best, I never heard anything in the news about a bad injury. Now, this is something I'm sure everyone will be talking about. Including this town.

My heart breaks for him and my brain worries.

I pull up the message I never answered and hover over it for a split second before opening it.

I don't think, I just type. My heart is in my hands.

Me: I hope you're okay. Please be okay.

I give myself another minute to relax, wiping my sweaty palms on my scrubs, and head into the emergency room for my night shift just hoping it goes a lot better than this day was.

Hoping that Mason is alright.

8 - Mason

My Dad's here.

The feeling of the scratchy hospital blanket is the only reminder that I'm awake. My mind is completely numb as is my body.

Out for the rest of the season.

The rest of the goddamn season. We were just two games away from the playoffs, the third seed in our conference. We were so fucking close. And now? I can't even lift my fucking arm. I need surgery and am out for at least three months.

It was hard not to go to a dark place at that moment. It was hard to concentrate on anything else besides the feeling of being tackled and feeling a tear. It was a gut-wrenching reminder that we're not invincible on that field no matter how much we feel like we are. I had seen teammates get bussed off the turf more times than I'd like, never picturing it'd be me.

But now it was.

"How are you feeling Mason?" Dr. Callahan was the specialty doctor for our team and had been on every injury case this season. He looked as sullen as I felt, both of us knowing what this means.

"What do you think?" I snap.

"Mason. Act like a grown-up." My father's voice cuts in and I grip the edge of the bed.

"Why are you even here? Huh?" I turn to him, my arm hooked up to the machines behind my bed restricting my access to turn my body fully. I ignore the sharp pain in my shoulder and the sling on my arm to look him dead in the eye.

"I don't want you here." I spit.

The doctor looks between my dad and me before stepping around to block my view from where my sad excuse of a father sits on the plastic chair.

"Okay, Mason. I can't begin to understand the emotions you're feeling right now but I can't have yelling and strain on your arm. We need to talk about the next steps and act fast." He slides a spare chair over. "Now, do you understand where we stand?"

He looks down at his clipboard and I lean back into the bed closing my eyes.

I'd rather be anywhere but here right now. Anywhere in the world.

"Yes," I say clenching my teeth together.

"Good. We will move forward with surgery on the shoulder." I shut my eyes as he says the words. Maybe if I don't watch him say it, it won't be real. But the pain every time I move is a reminder of exactly what is real and what isn't.

The Doc leaves the room, a solemn look on his face. I turn to my father who just looks down at his phone, typing away. He's got his usual business suit on and wears the same look on his face as always. The same monotonous and expressionless face. I wonder if he ever smiles.

Not to me.

"Marie is on her way now. I'll call your mother." He looks up and I turn away.

"Don't you even dare! Don't call her." I'd rather talk to this embarrassing excuse of a parent than one that decided I wasn't worth it.

"She is still your mother Mason. You need to grow up." I laugh at his pathetic statement and run my good hand over my face. My limbs feel heavier than normal and my thoughts are scrambled. The pain medications doing their job of numbing everything. Almost everything.

"Rich coming from you." I snap.

I know I'm acting like a grown baby. I know I'm being an asshole, but nothing feels right anymore. We were playing the best we ever had this season. Only lost three games and winning the rest.

Coach Hanson was not known for taking more risks than he could handle. He had built the New England Warriors from the ground up, picking his players selectively and decisively. He made no mistakes and took no unnecessary gambles.

Now I was a gamble. One I'm not sure he'd be willing to take.

"Enough of this. You'll get the surgery tomorrow morning before you risk letting the dislocation and tear set. I'm going to meet Marie in the city at a hotel. Call if you need me." He stands not making eye contact with me. His words are an empty promise, I know he wouldn't answer if I called. He was too busy with his work or handing Marie his black Amex card to turn his attention to me.

"Right." I sigh.

He waves goodbye, already half out the door and the second it closes behind him I take a breath.

I focus on my breathing and not the anxious thoughts that fill my mind. Darius had taught me a technique his therapist told him once, one that helped my breathing when I felt an attack coming. I focused on my toes and pictured them falling asleep. I continued all up my body to my head, all while picturing each body part along the way falling asleep.

It forced me to focus on just that. That and the feeling of complete relaxation.

It was all I could find solace in.

I am just reaching my shoulders when the door opens again. I turn expecting it to be my dad forgetting something but am met with a sad-looking Darius and Shawn behind him. They're dressed in their normal clothes but from the sweat and dirt on their skin, I can tell they didn't bother to shower before rushing here.

"What a way to spend Christmas Eve buddy." It's Shawn who speaks first, stepping around Darius who has barely moved from his spot at the door. He knows just how serious this is, he already knows what this means.

"Did you win?" I ask.

"We pulled through. The fourth quarter was rough without you man, our defense was the only thing keeping us afloat at that point." Darius says, stepping into the room completely.

I turn away from them.

Our second-string quarterback was a guy named Jasper Wright. He was good but young. Just like I was three years ago. I knew the feeling of being thrown into the game for the first time. It was a feeling of pure adrenaline and running off of instinct.

If I could stomach it, I'd watch the end of the game in a re-run to see how he did.

"What's the verdict, Jones?" Darius takes a seat.

"Out." I sigh. "I need surgery tomorrow morning. Then it's a three-month recovery. Three-month throw restriction." I list off the exact words Doc gave me an hour ago after his initial assessment of my injury.

"Fuck," Shawn turns. "Fuck fuck, fuck."

"Have you heard from Coach yet?" Darius is the one who asks.

"No." I can only assume the media and press are going crazy. I can only assume the coach is getting a phone call every second questioning whether or not his quarterback is out for the rest of the season. Instead of celebrating their win, they're stressing over an injury.

"Don't worry Mas, it'll be fine," Shawn says.

I try to believe him but that's just not the case. The case of the matter is I'm out and I will be for a long time. Instead of living at the high start of my early career, I'll be questioned for the next few years as a liability.

"Yeah, I'm sure." I lied.

They stay for the next hour or so before visiting hours are up. Everyone on the team is going home to spend time with their family before the next game. Home for the holidays. Something I am dreading.

I debated staying up here in Boston and finding a good rehab center that would help me through the recovery process, but that wasn't happening. My doctor and team representatives say I should go home with my family and recover there.

How do I tell them that's the opposite of recovery?

My phone lights up beside me on the table and I reach over.

"Fuck." The strain of the lean reaches my injured shoulder sending a jolt of pain down my back. I grab the phone as quickly as possible and prepare myself for the endless messages.

And I'm met with hundreds.

Every player on the team has sent me a message, saying how sorry they are and hope I'm okay. Distant relatives are questioning what happened and if I'm out for the season. I've been tagged in hundreds of Instagram posts wishing me well.

All of it makes me nauseous.

This isn't what I had planned. This isn't what I wanted.

I clear all my notifications and go to clear my messages when I catch one that stands out, and for a moment my numb heart beats again.

Del: I hope you're okay. Please be okay.

If I wasn't hooked up to a heart monitor I'd fear that my heart stopped. Seeing her again all those months ago was like a shock to my system, and I couldn't get her out of it. To this day I still go to bed thinking about that dinner, that almost kiss, and I can't sleep.

I know she feels guilty about not answering before. I know It's probably eating away at her inside because I know I'd feel the same. But she told me the truth, the truth being that she couldn't handle talking to me again if it meant nothing.

How do I tell her it means everything without scaring her away?

My fingers hover over the blank message bar before typing back.

Me: I'm okay.

I shut off my phone and shut out any unwelcome thoughts about my injury or how bad my shoulder hurts at this moment. Instead, I focus on Delilah and her smile. It always did make me feel better when I needed it the most.

9 - Delilah

He's okay.

But why doesn't that make me feel any better? Up until two months ago I had almost all but forgotten about his existence with the occasional reminder every time he played a home game that my dad and I would watch.

I was moving on, and now I felt as though I was stuck in mud gripping onto what could've been. Not to mention the reminder that he'd be coming home for his recovery, a very impending thought. The night before, I had seen in the news that he'd take up resting at home and then physical therapy with a specialized trainer at the local hospital.

The hospital I was employed at.

It's as if I was in some crazy storybook, someone was writing my life as a joke at this point.

"Did you check on room 208?" Tish pulls me from my impending thoughts. I look up at her and nod. "Yes, I'm heading out at ten. Need a ride?" Tish has been a friend from PA school and happened to do her residency years in town as well. She was from Pennsylvania and wanted to live in the ocean state for some as her mother once lived here.

"No thanks, Nick is picking me up!" Nick is just her friend, that's not so much just a friend. Everyone who knows her knows that fact, well except her. They met a year ago in town at a coffee shop and I had told her that couldn't be more book worthy of the start of a perfect love story.

She laughed in my face.

"You'll see," I told her. I knew it was only within the time they'd get together and when that day comes I will make my way down to the local grocery store, purchase a cake and write in big bold red letters: I Told You So.

"Okay. I'll see you tomorrow."

I make my way out to my car, cursing the cold weather and wishing I lived somewhere warmer. I did love this time of year when it came to the holidays but when the holidays are over it is just dreary, bare, and cold.

A reflection of how I feel.

I had promised to grab groceries for dad on the way home so I did just that. He claimed he was going to be making my favorite chicken noodle soup for no reason at all, just that he wanted to. Deep down I know that isn't true and he's just trying to make up for the disaster that was Christmas Eve dinner.

We still hadn't talked about what happened and it was better that way. Until he was ready to come to terms with mom's death in a way without breaking, it would be impossible to talk to him.

I still struggled daily with her loss. I see it everywhere, in everything I do. I see it when I'm cooking dinner and am reminded of how much she just hated to cook. I see it in her favorite movies that I pass when deciding what to watch.

I see her everywhere.

But she's not here.

I finish up the grocery shopping and rush home as safely as possible to soak up the warmth of my heated house. Once inside I put everything away and plan to do some studying and catching up on different things I was unsure of. I try to take notes on shift so that afterward I can do more research and get a more well-rounded understanding of what I'm seeing.

"Delilah you here?" My dad's voice breaks through the silence.

"My room," I answer by closing my laptop. He steps around the corner and through my open door.

"Clara is at the door." He says. I look at my phone to see no missed calls or text messages and head to the front door. Clara stands there in her snow jacket and signature red beanie wearing a guilty expression on her face.

This can't be good.

"You didn't call." I close the door behind her and follow her into the kitchen. "Everything okay?" It seems like every time Clara calls unannounced or in this case shows up unannounced there is going to be some sort of bad news.

"I wanted to see you. Plus I have something to tell you." She sits at the table and I follow suit.

"He's here." She gets straight to the point. "He flew in this morning and tomorrow he'll be at the hospital for his first check-in and to meet the doctors there." She reaches for my hand.

"Are you going to be okay?" I registered that she is talking to me.

"Yes, of course. It will just be weird." She nods her head at my answer.

How do you go to work like normal with the thought of your very famous, very injured ex, showing up whenever he needs a check-up? I almost want to break all the rules and find out his schedule but that'd lead me straight to unemployment.

"I know," she looks up at me. "You should talk to him, clear the air and check up on him. Considering he's going to be home for a while." She's right. After he had texted me he was alright. I knew that wouldn't be the last of our communication.

I need to see him. I need to tell him how awful I feel that he's out for the season and that I hope for him the best in his recovery.

That's it, nothing more.

"I think I will. I have a shift tomorrow anyway so I'm assuming I'll run into him." I will explain.

She nods her head and stands making her way to the white refrigerator in the corner of the kitchen to grab water.

"Is it soup night?" Clara smiles at me with a knowing look.

"What do you think?" I whisper and nod my head to the hallway where my dad is probably in his room doing something random. She makes her way back over to me, taking a seat.

"Have you guys talked?" Her voice is hushed and she turns to make sure we're alone.

"No. We never do. It's the same old, getting angry at one another and him saying something he doesn't mean and then pretending like it never happened." I steal her water and take a sip.

"One of these days you're going to have to actually sit down with him and explain that this coping and pretending like he doesn't hurt you, isn't going to last forever."

I know she's right and I know deep down I've been telling myself the same thing. The only problem is it's a lot easier said than done. The dad that I could talk to about anything with no worry of yelling or uncontrolled anger, died the second my mother did. He's only a shell of himself now.

"I know."

We spend the next few hours talking about random events and the newest gossip within the small town, and before I know it I'm going to bed and preparing to see Mason Jones again for the second time in just a few months.

—

It's been three hours into this mid-day shift and I already want to go home and sleep for 24 hours. After today I have three days off and I'm going to spend those three days sitting at home, sleeping, and doing absolutely nothing.

I have been avoiding the conversations that have wafted through the hospital about a certain visitor coming today. Someone who I knew very well.

As much as I've heard about Mason showing up, I haven't seen him. I'm assuming I'd know when he's here by the sheer amount of fangirling that is going on at the nurse's stations and breakrooms. Who can blame them really?

"I'm going on my break," I tell my PA and she nods, dismissing me. I had been shadowing Maddie for the last week and it's been as interesting as it is frustrating. I knew she meant well and she's an excellent teacher. She just can be challenging at times.

I take my break in my favorite spot in the back of the hospital. There is a small garden and in the summer even a nice little fountain. With the winter season in full effect, it's less visually appealing but there is a small greenhouse within the garden that no one really tends to besides the landscapers.

I found it within my first week of working here and ever since have come on my breaks or whenever I needed to relax. The stress of being in a hospital surrounded by the sick and dying weighs heavy on my heart and mental well-being.

It's almost a constant reminder of my mom.

Which is why I'm doing what I'm doing.

I'm almost at the door of the greenhouse, a hot coffee in one hand from the cafeteria and leftover soup in the other when I stop in my tracks. From where I stand outside I see a figure walking around through the glass door.

Except it's not just any figure, it's Mason.

His face is serious and he wears a black beanie on his head. I can tell from the way he stands that he's in pain and most definitely should not be walking. With that in mind, I push my way through the door and interrupt his very clear panic with my sentence.

"Mason? What are you doing here?" Seeing him again is like a breath of fresh air and like jumping in a frozen lake. Both of which are wake up calls.

He stills at my voice and his rosy cheeks from the heat and cold blare a light red. His eyes roam my blue scrubs and the items in my hands before meeting my eyes. And for the first time since seeing him through the glass, a small smile reaches his lips.

"Waiting for my appointment. What are you doing here?" He jokes and then I watch as he winces.

"Mason you really shouldn't be up and walking like this after surgery. Why don't you sit down." I point to the bench, concerned about his pain. He was probably bedridden for a few days after the surgery and should take it easy for a while.

"Okay, Dr. McKenna." He tries to lighten the mood but I can tell it does nothing in his head. His eyes are sad and his posture reads pain. For someone who always has to be strong and show leadership on the field, I can't imagine how hard it is for him.

"Very funny," I say.

We awkwardly stand there for a moment, neither of us knowing what to do. He finally moves to take a seat where I usually eat my lunch. When he's seated I opt for an old carton, turning it over to the flat side and taking a seat in the corner across from him.

"I can't believe you're a doctor Del. This is crazy." He tries to make conversation.

"Not a doctor. Still in PA school." I comment, opening up the warm soup that I heated up in the cafeteria on the way over. I take a small bite, overly aware of his eyes on me the entire time.

"Still. You're living your dream." He says it in a way like he wants me to remember it was my own dream. He's right, it was a dream of mine and still is. When we were together all I would do is talk about the fact I'm going to be a PA one day and he was going to go pro, and that I'd be the one to mend all his wounds.

I couldn't mend the wound of our breakup though.

"Yea." I give him a smile.

His eyes never leave my face and he watches me eat my lunch silently. We both look for things to talk about but then fall short, both of us settling into awkwardness.

"When's your appointment?" I ask after setting down my finished Tupperware.

"Now." He breathes out once and turns his head, clenching his jaw. "I'm not ready to face it all yet." He says honestly.

I didn't expect him to open up to me or even give me a glimpse into what he was thinking. I look down at his shoulder all bandaged up and in a sling.

"You don't have to face it all. You just have to face today." He slowly turns back to me after hearing my words and I suddenly think I've gone too far.

"You always knew what to say." He smiles over at me. "I've missed you."

There it is.

Again.

We're back to where we were two months ago when he visited town before his season. We're back to being strangers who miss each other. We're back to being ex-lovers who couldn't make it work.

"Mason." I sigh, turning my head away from his gaze. I need to leave before my feelings bubble out of my head and through my mouth. Before I say something I can't erase.

"You should get to the appointment. I'm sure they're all looking for you." He looks at me and shakes his head in disappointment.

Whether that be at my answer or my lack thereof. It doesn't matter.

"You're right." He then stands very slowly, wincing along the way. He's almost fully up when I watch him reach for the cart behind him for stability, but instead, it pushes away and he's thrown off balance.

Without thinking I rushed to his good side, throwing my shoulder under his armpit and accepting some of his weight, preventing a fall. We both freeze in shock at what almost just happened and I'm reminded of how much larger he is than me.

"Shit." He swears, gaining his balance back and gripping my waist to help. "Fuck, thank you Del. I just, I just can't-," he turns his head away from me.

"It's alright Mason. You just had shoulder surgery and your body needs to recover. Let me get a wheelchair okay?" I say softly, doing my best to ignore the way his arm feels around my waist and the familiar scent of his cologne.

"No. I'm fine, I can walk." He stubbornly stands straight and I step away from him. "I don't need a wheelchair." I give him a look that says bullshit and turn to the greenhouse door.

"Mason, asking for help and knowing when you need it are the first steps of your recovery. You need to rest your shoulder and you most definitely can not fall. You will sit in a wheelchair and I will wheel you to your appointment or you will sit here and not get better." I huff out, not knowing where the sudden burst of anger and confidence came to say that.

Mason looks just as shocked as I do and I know for a fact I overstepped now. I just can't stand watching him in pain and stubbornly refusing the help I know would relieve it.

I wait for him to yell back at me or tell me I have no right but instead, I watch as his lips creep up into a smirk.

"I've missed your fire Del girl."

10 - Mason

She's so pretty when she's angry at me.

If I wasn't so concentrated on ignoring the sting of pain in my shoulder, I'd be coming up with a way to keep her that way. I can't stand it when she looks at me with pity or concern, I don't want her to worry.

I want to keep her being bossy.

I admire the way she acts and how relaxed she is in her element. Her job, her city, her small greenhouse. Even as I watched her eat the soup silently, I studied her and all I missed these four years.

"I'm going to get a wheelchair." She rolls her eyes and takes a step in the direction of the hospital but I don't miss the way she fights a smile.

I sit down on a cold bench and pull out my phone to text the boys an update. Both Darius and Shawn have been on my ass since the flight home trying to convince me to use this time to talk to Delilah.

If I remember correctly, Darius said exactly: "Get your shit together and fix things."

Coming home I knew I'd run into Delilah. I knew that we'd see each other more than we had all these years, and I knew it'd be awkward. She's made it clear since the moment I saw her again that what we had, is over.

It may be completely over for her but for me I still held onto the small memories of the past and the what ifs like it was a lifeline.

"Alright, sit down." Her crisp voice pulls me from my thoughts and I look up at her stern face.

She means all business and I can't help but smile at her fierceness. She always did have a fire in her, always so strong and independent even when she didn't have to be. Like now, she doesn't have to be here doing this for me on her break. She doesn't have to pretend like this isn't awkward for the both of us, but she does anyway.

"Yes ma'am." She blushes at the ma'am.

I stand and then slowly turn my back to her, sliding down into the wheelchair while being careful not to hit my elbow or move my arm.

After surgery, I was bedridden for three days, and not allowed to move at all. It was the worst three days of my life. For the last ten years of my life, all I've done is move, go, and work. Sitting still in one place for long periods was never in my cards.

"Don't call me that." She clicks the brakes free and pushes forward.

"Fuck," she grunts at the weight of me. "I forgot how big you were." I can tell she meant for those words to be a whisper but I caught them and turned to face her.

"Don't. Even. Say. It." Her face is completely flushed now and I save her the embarrassment of a lame "that's what she said" joke and enjoy the ride through the bright white hospital that will be my living hell for the next three months.

"How's your dad holding up?" She asks.

"He's fine. He's at work." Normally I would hate the idea of talking about my dad, but I know she means well. She knew my parents before they fell apart, she knew their dynamic and the man my dad used to be.

"Is he the one driving you to these visits?" She pushes the elevator button and we wait for it to come. "Or is Marie doing it?"

"He drove me today, but I'll uber the rest of them." She steps beside me and looks down at me.

"You're going to uber? Here? To your appointment... with a recovering shoulder?" Disbelief coats every word and I see the confusion on her face and scrunched eyebrows.

"Yep." I look away.

"Why? He can't?" We make it into the elevator.

"No, he can. I'd rather run a mile naked in the middle of town than have him drive me Del." Just the drive over here had me questioning every decision in life.

He can't go a minute or two without talking about work or talking about football. All he does is pretend to care for the time being and then forget I exist the next.

It's the same cycle over and over again.

"I'm sure the town would love that." She jokes and pushes me through the open doors on level three, making our way down the hallway.

We come to a stop in a small waiting room that's almost completely empty. Just two people sit together on the chairs by the reception desk.

"Would you?" I say.

She stops pushing and I hear her catch her breath.

"I should have let you walk." She murmurs.

I'm glad she didn't. Talking like normal between us is the only sane thing that's happened to me in the past week. Hearing her voice and having her understand what I'm going through without even needing to tell her about it is a blessing in disguise.

She locks the wheelchair and I take it as my cue to stand again. I hate to admit how right she was with it because the second I stand completely and stretch up, my shoulder stings in pain. My entire upper body has been sore since the surgery and I have a feeling it won't change anytime soon.

"Well, you're good to go. Good luck." She goes to turn but before she can I reach out with my left hand to stop her.

"Thank you. Really." I mean it.

She looks up at me and I want to frame the moment. I want to pretend like we're freshmen in college again and we're both still each other's best friends. I want to pretend like life didn't happen and that the real world isn't a piece of shit.

I want to pretend we're the same Del and Mason from college.

"Of course. You need to listen to your doctors and rest. The sooner you do the sooner you can start throwing again." She looks so concerned it makes my heart beat faster.

"I know." I watch as she scans her eyes over my face and chest. Pausing at the sling and then back up to my eyes.

"Okay. Good luck in there, I have to go now." Before I can answer she turns around and high-tails it out of the waiting room.

I watch her walk away, her red hair in her wake. She doesn't turn back once and the second she disappears from view a random sense of loneliness overcomes me. It's like she can make someone feel as if they've never been alone in their life whenever in her presence.

Shortly after she leaves my name is called to be brought in and I meet with my doctor. She's an older lady and I recognize her from when I was younger. She, like everyone else in this town, gushed about how proud she was of me for making it big in this small town.

I never really know how to handle big compliments or sentiments like those so I always say thank you and that I appreciate all the love from here.

She goes over my pain and prognosis for the next few months. For now, it's going to be a lot of resting and not a lot of physical therapy. Physical training will come around six weeks later and until then she wants me to give it as much time as possible to heal.

When we're done I make my way back to the waiting room and take a seat.

I promised Marie I'd call my dad for the ride home, but at this moment I just want to be left alone.

Coach has checked up on me almost daily along with my other teammates but I know he's not happy with the fact I'm out. It's not any coach's dream to lose their quarterback a game before the playoffs start. He knew as well as I did that the odds didn't look good and that the team would be questioned and doubted for the rest of the road to the Superbowl.

"Mason?" I look up to a woman approaching me with a wheelchair. She's got brown hair and brown eyes and her smile is wide and bright.

"Delilah sent me. Said you would need a lift back down after your appointment. She's stuck with a patient at the moment so she asked if I could grab you instead." I don't know whether to laugh or cry at that moment.

Laugh at the fact my ex-girlfriend is just as stubborn as I remember or cry over the fact I can't even walk around a hospital without risking re-injury and furthering my no-game time.

"Thanks." I take a seat and stuff my pride far down my chest.

The ride down the elevator and out to the main lobby is far less enjoyable without a familiar redhead to keep me company. Tish is nice and makes small talk to fill the silence. I offer to sign a piece of paper for her friend and she tells me how he's a huge fan.

Before I know it we're in the lobby and I'm thanking her.

I'm careful to walk my way back outside into the cold air. I scan the quiet lot and even duller surroundings. One thing I hated about being home for holidays or having to visit dad, was the weather and the entire town was a depressing gray dull in the winter months.

"Call your Dad." I turn my head at the intrusion of a body beside me.

Delilah looks up at me flustered and out of breath as if she ran all the way here. Her chest rises and falls and my eyes rise and fall with it.

I look away immediately.

"Call your dad Mason. Please don't sit out here in the cold or call an uber that will probably take thirty minutes to get here because we live in the middle of nowhere." She reaches her hand out.

"Call him."

I stare at her fingers that wrap around my arm, her fingernails painted a chipped red.

"Why do you care so much, Del? You made it clear that you wanted your space. I don't get why you're being so nice now." I study her reaction.

She looks taken back and drops her hand. I instantly miss her touch and regret the words that left my mouth. I want to beg her to put her hand back.

"That's not fair Mason. You're hurt, you were one of my closest friends. I care about you." Her cheeks warm in a blush once more but my brain and heart catch onto the word friends.

It breaks a little.

"Friends huh? That's what you remember?" I don't mean for it to come out rude but it does.

It's been almost four years and she's deducted what we had as friends? Is this all just pity, is it all just a guilty conscience?

She shakes her head. "Stop it, Mason, don't do that." Her eyes meet mine again.

"You know what, fine. Don't call your Dad, or do. I'm going back to work." She turns on her heels back towards the direction of the entrance and for the second time today, she walks away from me.

And with her, she takes my hurtful words and leaves behind an even bigger hole in my sorry excuse for a heart.

11 - Delilah

I brush off my encounter with Mason and trudge through the rest of the shift. I knew most people became irritable when injured, facing all sorts of physical and mental battles. But, it was never an excuse to be rude to someone else.

I know he didn't mean to, I know it came out wrong. I'm not even mad at him.

If anything the whole exchange just confirmed that I needed to stay away while he got his shit together. Give him space to navigate his new normal for the next few months and keep my overbearing self away.

I didn't have trouble keeping my mind off everything because as soon as I got home I got my period and after years of gaslighting myself and belittling my pain, I took it seriously.

I have been struggling with painful periods since the beginning of high school.

At first, I just thought it was normal and everyone else felt the same as I do. Growing up all you hear is how older women would just "suck it up" and get on with their day. Imagine my shock when I found out in fact I could not just suck it up but rather had my fair share of emergency room visits.

It started small at first with painful cramping and heavy bleeding, but it only progressed each period. Now I'm usually bedridden for the first two days with nausea, sweating, and extreme pain.

So tonight, when the first feeling of the onslaught of my upcoming period showed up in my lower stomach I prepared to most likely be out tomorrow.

I hate explaining to people why I couldn't do things and for the first few years, I'd make up random excuses and say it was something else entirely but that just wasn't true.

I shouldn't have to sugarcoat what I'm going through at the expense of others and whether or not they feel comfortable with hearing me say I have painful periods.

"You okay hun?" My dad peaks his head around the corner from where I lean against the counter of the kitchen waiting for my food to heat up in the microwave.

"Yea I'm good." I smile reassuringly at him, not wanting him to worry.

"Okay well, I'm heading to bed. You get some rest." He smiles at me one more time and then turns down the dark hallway.

I wonder if he talked to his therapist today. I knew he had an appointment next week but he usually was only this talkative and empathetic after a session with his therapist. I wish he was always like this. I know it will be within time.

I grab my leftovers, and my giant bottle of water and make my way to my bedroom. My bed is warm and welcoming with my heating pad placed just right and a movie cued up on the screen.

I spend the next couple of hours unwinding, watching a random thriller movie on Netflix before calling it a night.

The next morning I'm not so lucky in having a repeat of my relaxing night. I wake up with that familiar feeling of uncomfortableness and tight pain in my lower abdomen, knowing it's going to be a long day.

I had gone to several different doctors who all gave me the same answer—endometriosis.

It's a weird sort of comfort because I'm glad I got my answer but it's not a very detailed one. They say it's very broad and it is. There are tons of symptoms and I happen to check the boxes of many.

I would fight it day by day.

I turn over in a lazy haze to take some pain meds and drink a glass of water but for the majority of the morning, I fade in and out of sleep.

I'm woken up by the sound of a phone ringing. Sitting up I wince at the tightness and reach for my phone.

"Hello?" My voice is scratchy and dry so I drink more water.

"Delilah? Are you okay?" It's Mason, his voice quivering in worry.

Why is he wondering if I'm okay?

"Yes? Why?" I take a breath.

"Well I tried calling you last night to apologize for being so– well curt with you yesterday. I knew you were only trying to help, but you didn't answer your phone. I figured you were probably giving me the cold shoulder like

I deserve but then I texted you again today a ton and now I feel like a total idiot because it sounds like you just woke up and I'm over here making myself look—" I cut him off with a laugh.

"Mason, relax. It's fine. Thank you for apologizing." He sounded truly panicked and If I wasn't in so much pain at the moment I'd be reeling in it.

"Okay. But, are you sure you're good? You don't sound good." He says.

Wow, thank you, Mason.

Rule number one, maybe don't remind your ex-girlfriend who you're trying to be on good terms with how awful she sounds at the moment?

"Thank you for that charming reminder." I turn over, bringing my legs up to my chest. "But, I'm fine just feeling a little under the weather." I take several deep breaths as another wave of cramps followed by nausea passes.

"Can I call you another time?" I can't focus, I'd rather dissect whatever this call means at less painful time in my life.

"Del, do you need anything?" There goes that nickname and that worry.

Shouldn't I be the one worrying for him? I mean, he's the one with the broken shoulder!

"I'm fine. You need to rest too." I say even though I want to ask him why he cares, that didn't end well earlier being on the receiving end. I guess it goes without saying at this moment and every moment since we've seen one another again, feelings are still there—feelings of worry, concern, and curiosity.

I don't think they ever truly went away.

He takes a moment and I can practically hear him thinking hard about what to say next. I take the time to mute so I can turn around and readjust my heating pad while groaning out loud, saving myself his questions if he hears.

"Is it, um, is it your period?" I go still and I feel my cheeks heat up even warmer than they already were.

For a moment I almost forgot how I had spent the majority of my new adult life with the man on the other end of the phone. How he held me those nights when the pain was unbearable. How he gave me both back and lower pelvic massages that he had learned from youtube just for me.

Great now my heart hurts on top of everything else.

"Yes," I whisper. He doesn't reply right away but I don't feel embarrassed for saying it.

He knows.

"I'm sorry Del. I remember how hard those were for you. If you need anything just, well, just text me okay? Or call. I'll be there." I couldn't help the one lone tear that dropped from my eye.

I can't help but feel overly emotional about this whole ordeal. I'm so confused about him being back, so out of sorts. I don't know how to feel anymore.

"Thank you, Mason. I'll be okay. I'm gonna go now, see you around." I drop my phone on my bed next to my pillow.

"Alright, feel better soon. Bye." I press the red button the second his voice disappears.

I remove my comforter and sit in a weird position to relieve my back pain.

It feels good to have someone worry for me like that. I know I have my friends and my dad but someone who was once... more. It's making my chest ache and my head hurt to think about so I try not to.

About halfway through the seemingly too long of a day I manage to text my friends to let them know I am alive and okay. Tish wishes me well and Clara offers to come by later with a good attitude and a back massage.

I don't decline.

I manage to get to a point by dinner where I can sit up in bed and not feel completely lightheaded, just in time for Clara and Ryan to come through my bedroom door. Just seconds before I heard them saying hi to my dad.

"There's my strong best friend." Clara smiles bubbly and Ryan closes the door behind her. They're both dressed casually and have convenience store bags on their wrists.

"What did you buy?" I try to take a peak inside but I can't see from where I sit up against my bed frame.

"I know you hate the whole stereotypical idea of craving chocolate and chips but you can't help what your body's craving. I brought them for when you feel better tomorrow." Clara sets them by my nightstand and I thank her.

"I brought nips. For when you're feeling a whole lot better." Ryan winks at Clara's scoff and then turns to me. "Fireball to warm the soul." I laugh softly to not disturb my body's current peace and thank them both.

"Mason called me today." I say. Clara almost chokes on the chip she's eating and Ryan raises her dark eyebrows in surprise.

I'm almost positive Ryan is a natural brunette but she's had black hair as long as I've known her with Clara. It suits her.

"Really? Was it about yesterday?" I had filled them in on what happened after my conversation outside the hospital with Mason, they were less than pleased.

"Yea, he apologized and then proceeded to worry about me because he heard how tired I was through the phone. He asked if it was my period because he remembered how tough they were when we were together." I recall his worry and it makes my chest tighten again.

"I'd say that's sweet but I'm mad at him," Clara concludes but I see the smile working her way onto her face. Ryan rolls her eyes and turns to me.

"That was nice of him. Glad he apologized. How do you feel about him being back and all that? Is it weird?" She asks while brushing her hands through her girlfriend's hair.

"It is weird." I think. "It's like we're in this world of limbo. Worrying for each other but at the same time realizing we don't have to anymore? I'm not really sure what's going on to be completely honest." I say.

It's true, I have no idea. But in a strange way, I like it.

"Could you see yourself getting back with him?" Clara asks.

"No," I say quickly, too quickly. They both look at me with knowing eyes but don't say anything.

We can't and we won't. He's going back to pro ball after recovery and I'll be accepting any job offer I can when I graduate. It's not logical to start anything.

"Whatever you say, love bugs. Now flip over, magical hands time." Clara wiggles her fingers and Ryan snorts.

"Babe, maybe not the innuendos while your girl is in the room." She says light-heartedly.

Clara is actually a massage therapist and has been for several months now. She works at the local massage therapy place in the town center and gets all the good gossip.

"I love you." Clara leans over to give Ryan a kiss and I look away giving them privacy. I take another sip of water before turning around on my stomach, breathing through the pain.

"Alright, let's get you some relief." She says it and I can tell she didn't think before because she laughs at the double meaning and I just shake my head.

"BABE!" Ryan laughs and it's a good sound.

All of us laugh together and take the seriousness out of this day and this pain. It was a good warm feeling and I grasped onto it as Clara's cold fingers made contact with my burning skin.

~~~

12 - Mason

"How's the pain today?" The doctor's white coat scratches at my exposed skin and I shift uncomfortably in my seat.

"It's okay." It wasn't. It's been another week of resting and now I'm back for my weekly check-up with the doc hoping that the weeks go by like seconds that tick down until I can throw again. I've been going out of my mind, my body begging to let it get back to its rigorous routine.

I've done nothing but sit at home and get sucked into my phone. I read all the headlines with my name in them and instantly regret it. They're all questioning my recovery and my ability to bounce back. The comments on social media have been coming in by the hundreds every day, some wishing me well others hoping I die and don't come back.

Overall I'm doing really well.

"Well just keep up the rest and in a couple of weeks we can reevaluate your motion ability." She smiles a dull smile, a reminder of how depressing the whole idea of this is.

She finishes up the appointment and I breathe in the hospital's stale air the second the heavy door closes behind me. The right side of my body is extra sore today from the lack of sleeping well and every step I take brings a shooting pain to my shoulder.

I ignore it.

The vibrating in my pocket distracts me from the surprised eyes in the hallway as I pass.

"Hello?" I answer without looking at who's calling.

"Mason, Marie, and I are going up to Boston for the weekend. Don't bother waiting around. See you Monday." My dad's voice is firm and uninterested like calling me is a chore.

"Alright." He hangs up after that and it dampened my mood even more.

I am thinking of getting a small apartment close to the hospital so I don't have to spend another minute in the same household as that man. I can do this alone and I will do this alone.

The elevators ahead are to my left and in the middle of the open floor are a few tables and a small coffee bar along the back wall. This must be a small break area. I scan the tables unconsciously and stop completely when a flash of familiar red hair catches my attention.

Delilah sits alone with a hot cup of coffee on the metal table. She's engrossed in some fantasy book and by the biting of her lip, I can tell it's a good part.

The last time I talked to her was over the phone to apologize for my curt behavior. I was an asshole to her and she didn't deserve to be snapped at after just trying to help. When I called I expected her to be upset and cold with me but was met with her breathy pain-filled voice.

I make my way over to the table and her head whips up, looking surprised. She smiles at me and closes her book, dog-earing the corner of the page. That has to be some sort of crime in the book world.

"Hey," I say.

"Hi. How's the recovery going." A light blush of pink coats her pale cheeks and it makes my heart skip a beat.

God, I feel like a teenager in love again.

"Good, just had a check-up. More rest it is." I shuffle to the left as someone passes. "May I?" I point to the open metal chair across from her. Her eyes follow where I point and she nods.

"Good book?" I ask, once seated. My shoulder thanked me for it.

"Yea. I haven't read fantasy in a while so..." Her voice trails off and she clears her throat. "I'm just on my break so I don't have much time. Did you want to talk about something?" She furrows her brows and I want to run my thumb over the concerned crease.

"Oh, no. I can go. Just, again I'm sorry for how I acted the other day outside. You were just trying to help." I look her in the eyes.

"It's okay Mason. You don't have to apologize again." She gives me a warm smile and looks away.

"Alright well, have a good rest of your shift." I go to stand, secretly wishing I had something else to talk to her about so I could get more time with her.

I don't know what's going on between us, I don't know what line we're treading on but I know I don't want it to end.

"Excuse me?" I turn my head to the left where a blonde woman is holding out a paper and pen. "Do you mind signing this for me? My husband is a huge fan!" She smiles wide flashing her very white teeth.

I quickly signed her paper and thanked her. Looking back to where Delilah is I'm met with an empty chair and a tiny dribble of coffee left on the table. She's gone again.

—-

"I was thinking of coming down the next chance I get. That's cool with you?" Darius is on the other line and I'm trying to shave with my left hand. I'm already weaker than normal so throwing in my non-dominant hand makes the task even harder.

"Only if you can dude. You guys gotta be real busy." I rinse the razor in the sink, watching the tiny hairs and foam go down the drain.

"Never too busy for you man. Me and Cas can come to see you. I'll bring beer and bad advice." I laughed at his response and cut my cheek in the process.

"Fuck–," I drop the razor and reach for toilet paper to wipe the blood.

"I gotta go, man, shaving is my worst enemy at the moment." I sit on the edge of the tub, careful not to move my shoulder much.

"Alright. Keep in touch. See you soon." I hang up and drop my head.

FOUR YEARS AGO (;))

"Mason, pleaaase. I've watched you do it for like two years now." Del slipped between my arms, my hands gripping the sink. She wiggles herself into the cage my arms formed, our bodies close enough to touch now.

I smile at her.

"No baby. I'd like to live." I joke with her.

She swats at my chest and then raises her brow, smirking.

"Fine, I'll watch." She turns and for a moment I think she's telling the truth but the feel of her body pressing back into mine tells me all I need to know.

Her ass makes contact with my pelvis and I shake my head at her antics.

"Go ahead." She smiles a fake innocent smile at me through the mirror.

Fine, two can play this game. I pick up the razor and lean forward enough so that her back is completely pushed up against my shirtless chest. She gasps at the feeling of my left hand snaking around her waist, gripping her side.

I lean my head down so that it's parallel to hers, brushing my lips against her neck without fully touching, smiling at the hitch in her breath.

"What are you doing?" She turns and I'm already so close that our mouths are a centimeter apart.

"Nothing." I lean in to kiss her nose before turning back to the mirror and grabbing the shaving cream. She watches me closely, bodies pressed together and I think to myself I never want to shave alone again.

I drag the razor carefully over the stubble of my beard, watching her watch me. I notice the way her eyes zone in my hand and her breathing seems to pick up.

Naughty Del.

"You okay there?" I smirk, rinsing off the blade.

She nods her head so I continue. We spend the next five minutes teasing one another through our eyes. I can tell she's turned on and I know she can feel how hard I am through my sweatpants, but none of us act on it.

Some sort of sick foreplay this is.

"Let me." She turns quickly, grabbing the dry facecloth from the railing. She reaches up and wipes my face free of the leftover shaving cream. I'm hyperaware of everything she's doing, every part of her that's touching me. It feels amazing, everything about her is amazing.

She drops the towel and looks up at me through her long lashes and all my control snaps.

I grip the sides of her face and pull her lips to mine, needing her as close as possible. I back her up, lips moving with hers, and lift her onto the sink. She smiles into my mouth and drags her teeth over my lip. It shoots heat straight down my spine and I moan into her mouth.

Fuck.

"You're gonna kill me Del." I drag my hands down the side of her body, loving the way goosebumps follow in a trail of desire.

"Never." I rush our lips back together and grip the back of her hair all while she works the strings of my sweatpants.

Yea, never shaving alone again.

13 - Delilah

I think I've officially gone crazy.

It's the only logical explanation for why I'm on the doorstep of Mason's childhood home clutching a Barnes and Noble bag. The only logical reasoning for why I feel like I need to be here doing this is—well there is none.

I came to the conclusion approximately two hours ago after my shift ended that I wasn't going to sit by and watch someone I used to know to go down a dark path. His whole demeanor at the hospital screamed dark and gloomy, the look in his eyes losing the light they always had.

I know it's just a shoulder injury and he'll bounce back, but I can't help but feel like he has no one. Maybe I'll hurt myself in the end, maybe this will end badly but at this moment it feels like the right thing to do.

I watched my mother go to her lowest surrounded by people who loved her. Taking away pain isn't always possible but being there for someone can make all the difference.

I grip the bag and wrap my knuckles around the large front door.

Mr. Jones always was one for style and expressing his wealth. If his mansion wasn't a reflection of it, then it was the well-manicured lawn even in the dead of winter. He always was a force to be reckoned with whenever I was in the same room as him.

I'm ripped from my thoughts at the creak of the door opening and a very shirtless Mason standing there. I watch as several different emotions pass through his face, finally settling on surprise.

"What happened?" I ask, zeroing in on the blood on his cheek and the towel in his hand.

I realize that maybe that shouldn't have been my first words to him, seemingly stunned to silence.

"Uh, shaving." He clenches his jaw and shakes his head. "Are you okay? Why are you here?" He asks, looking down at the bag in my hand and raising his brows.

"Can I come in?" My heart is racing as the words tumble from my lips.

I haven't been in this house in years. The last time was for Marie's birthday. I still remember that night and the way we stayed up well past two am talking about our futures.

I think it was the last time before everything ended.

"Uh, yea. Of course." He stands back, still confused.

I pass him in the doorway, hyperaware of the heat radiating off his naked chest, and force myself to look anywhere but the well-worked muscle stretching with his every move. His arm was still in the sling and I mentally thanked him for doing what was right.

"I just thought you could use something to keep your mind busy." I trail my eyes over the pristine furniture and the empty feeling that always follows it.

A house but not a home.

"Del, you didn't need to do that. But thank you." Mason comes around from where I stand in the middle of the entryway. He takes the bag from my tight grip and we both pause at the contact. His fingers brush mine, sending sparks up my arm.

Abort.

"Um, yea. After seeing you today I figured the recovery process can get pretty lonely." I step back, dropping my hand.

"A good book can always help." I smile hoping it covers the anxiety I feel at being so close to him. My heart is racing faster than normal and all I can smell is that rich cologne he's worn for years.

"I'm sure you're right." I follow him down the hallway and into the large kitchen. He stops at the marble island dropping the paper bag on the white top. He takes a seat at the stool and I watch as he winces.

"Is your Dad home?" I haven't heard any voices besides ours and I noticed only one car in the expansive driveway.

"No, he and Marie went up to Boston for the weekend." He looks disinterested at the thought of it.

There is a moment of awkward silence. The both of us just stared at one another, him still shirtless. I look over his face and catch the blood that's not scabbed over. His hair is damp and I'm assuming he just got out of the shower.

My mind goes somewhere south.

"Trouble shaving?" I tease, taking a step towards him and crossing my arms over my chest in comfort. His eyes follow my movements and the air seems to thicken between us.

This new normal is uncharted territory.

"Mhm," he rolls his eyes. "Just another everyday task I can no longer do." He shakes his head.

"Let it grow out. No need to cause more harm than good." The sound of a car driving past fills the dead air.

"You always did like me with a small beard, didn't you?" He teases, eyes finding my wide ones. He says it as a joke but we both know there is more to it than that. I stand there shaking my head and he tilts him as if to say— remember?

I don't answer him, instead, I take a seat next to him at the island forcing his body to turn and face me. Our knees touch and I ignore the feeling just like I have been all night.

"Aren't you cold?" I point to his naked chest, his eyes following my direction.

"Well, I wasn't really expecting a visitor to shave." He jokes. "Next time let me know when you're on your way so I can put on my best suit." He winks and I look away training not to laugh.

"And," his voice drops. I look back over at him and his eyes are on mine, a smirk on his lips. "It's not like you haven't seen it before." Okay, not cool. My stomach drops at his words and I feel as though the temperature in the room suddenly went up several degrees.

"Delilah." He's serious, voice just above a whisper.

This was a bad idea. Coming here, trying to be a good person. I'm in over my head here, feeling things I haven't felt in years. Seeing him and being near him is a reminder of my own body and mind in what we lost. I try to ignore it but it's impossible.

"Mason." I find myself daydreaming.

He looks pained like he wants to say something but doesn't know how. Instead of talking, he reaches forward and before I know it his fingers are caressing the skin on my cheek. The feeling is like none other, It feels like a breath of fresh air and agony all in one. I lean into his open hand, allowing myself a moment of serenity.

"You're so beautiful." He's even closer now, his breath touching my face—minty and fresh.

I lean back, clearing my throat and snapping us both from the trance of desire. I wished for moments like this. The year of our breakup, I wished and prayed that I could feel his touch again. That we could be together again.

"Sorry," he stands and I follow. Both of us stand there awkwardly, so close yet miles between us. I want to say more, he wants to say more. Neither of us knows where to start.

"It's alright," I say because it is. Pretending like we both don't care for one another will never work. Gone are the feelings of love and relationship, what sits between us now is familiarity and distance.

I watch as he walks to the glass refrigerator, pulling out a bottle of water.

"Well, I think I should go. Just wanted to drop off the book. And Mason," I move towards him. He turns to give me his full attention, his brown hair now a bit drying in his signature messy curls. His chest moves up and down with his uneven breaths, the white strap of his sling reflecting in the refrigerator light.

"Yea," he shuts the door.

"If you need someone to talk to, I'm here. It can get hard being at the lowest point during recovery. No one should do it alone." I say sincerely.

He smiles a full smile, teeth showing and everything.

"Thank you Del." He steps forward. "I'm going to hug you now, is that ok?" I debated it for less than a second before taking a step forward.

He opens his left arm up and I lean into him, careful of his right shoulder. We both sink into each other. I remember to breathe as his fingers skim my back. He feels different and the same all in one. His body is clearly a reflection of all the hard work he's done in those past four years, but the feeling of warmth and the smell of his cologne is a reminder of what I once called home.

"Of course it's okay. What are friends for?" He stiffens next to me before recovering. We both break the hug taking a step back.

"So we're friends?" He smiles but it's not a full one.

I know he wants me to say more but that's all we can and will be.

"Yea. I guess we are." His hands curl into a fist before relaxing again, clearly not the answer he was hoping for.

"Good because I've missed you. And I could totally use a reading partner." I laugh lightly, thankful at the break in the tension.

I'm at the door and pulling it open when I turn around again. He's still shirtless and I'm still focusing on breathing.

"Well, I'll leave you to shave. Try not to lose too much blood." I joke and he laughs.

It's a deep laugh, a rumble that vibrates through the air.

"Drive safe okay? Text me when you get home." He points at me, to be serious. "Don't forget." I smile.

"I won't." I turn away, making my way back to my car. I don't turn around but I know he's waiting until I get in safely and lock the doors. Something he's always done and I asume will never stop.

I make sure to wave in the direction of the door as I pass, keeping my eyes on the driveway.

I don't know how to feel about what just happened and what I just did but I think it feels good. I think I can be friends with my ex-boyfriend who's super attractive, kind and very famous.

I could totally do this.

I think.

14 - Mason

"Just ask her out, Man." Darius and Shawn stand in my backyard tossing a football back and forth. They had the weekend off and drove down to visit me, claiming I was missing their pretty faces.

Losers.

"It's not like that Shawn. She's," I pause and drop my head into my hands. "She's special. She's not just some random girl I think is hot at the bar, she's more than that. All she's willing to give is friendship, and I'll take it."

Delilah's unexpected visit last week confirmed all of my questions. Nothing was going to happen between us, nothing would ever again. She called me her friend and told me she'd be here for me, as a friend. If that wasn't clearer than being written down I don't know what is.

"Well, what do you want?" Shawn drops down onto the bench next to me while Darius leans against the pillar in front of us.

What do I want? I'd like a healed shoulder for starters. Maybe a Dad who loved me and a Mom who cared enough to be in her son's life. Maybe to go back in time and figure out where it all went wrong with Delilah, figure out what I could've done.

"A lot." I settled on it.

"If you like her, and still have feelings for her then fight for her." Darius looks at me seriously. "Life is too short and too unpredictable to not tell someone you love them." He shuffles his feet and I take what he said to heart.

The word love sent tingles down my spine and a cold feeling across my chest.

"I don't know about love man, it's been years." I shake my head and stand. "I guess just being around her again has opened up a can of memories and feelings I thought I fucking buried. Deep." I take a breath.

I should spend my time worrying about my recovery and whether or not I'll still have a spot on the team when I'm healthy. I should be doing everything in my power to get better sooner. Instead, I'm worrying over a girl I fell in love with years ago who's made it very clear what's done is buried.

"Whatever you say. I just think that you've been given another chance, another opportunity to be around her again. You're older, maybe wiser but I wouldn't give you that much," Shawn laughs at Darius' words. "But you're definitely not the same man you were when she last saw you. You're adults now, and you have this chance."

A chance? A chance to what? I wasn't stupid enough to believe for a minute that Delilah would take me back as I am, in the circumstances we are in. I'd be leaving again, just like I had to the first time we were in this position.

"Stop worrying so much and just live." Darius steps up to me and taps on my good shoulder. "You're getting wrinkles hot shot." I shove my left fist into his chest as threateningly as possible with the zero strength I have.

I have to admit it was nice having them around again. It'd been weeks since I'd been away from the team and leaving behind all that crazy to come here in the middle of nowhere, was a change.

"Can't say I missed your very insightful advice D, but I do appreciate you guys coming down." I make my way back into the house, the frigid air reminding me I'm wearing nothing but a hoodie.

"Couldn't leave you without my presence for long." Shawn teases, taking a seat on the open island. I hand him a cold beer and pass one to D. We sit in silence for some time, watching the TV that's playing Monday night football.

"Hey, didn't you say there is a bar in town? Why don't we stop there for a few drinks, and get out of the house?" Shawn asks, setting his beer on the marble table.

"I'm not really up for that shit right now." I step aside and head for the living room. "But you two feel free, all the locals will be there. I'm sure they'd love to meet you and get some autographs." I sit on the empty couch.

"No no no, you're coming with us. Get up, throw on something decent and meet us in the car." Darius follows Shawn to the front door. "I'll start it up so It's not fucking freezing." The sound of the front door closing tells me he's serious.

Darius moves around the couch to where I sit, blocking my view of the TV.

"Are you supporting this?" I nod to the front door.

"Yep, let's go out. I could use a night out with my friend." He wiggles his brows and I almost throw up.

"You guys make me sick. Give me ten." He laughs as I make my way down the hall toward my room.

—-

Old Joe's is packed for a Monday night. There are swarms of people around the bar and some on the table tops. I scan the crowd wishing I was anywhere but here. The stares and whispers were an added headache to my already throbbing shoulder.

"I'll grab a table," I tell the boys and head over to an empty one. I smile as I pass familiar faces and say hi to some fans. A couple of girls stop me and ask for an autograph and a picture, I oblige even though I just want to sit.

Finally, I reach the table alone waiting for D and Shawn to bring some beers. I reach for my phone and check up on my emails which are swarmed with back-and-forth threads between my agent, manager, and officials I've never met in my life.

Everything was in shambles, the coaches focused on the playoffs and their actual functioning players, not concerned with the one who was fucked up for the season. I tried not to worry about the words flashing across my screen— how long?, meeting to discuss, Coach won't like that.

All words drove me half insane and that feeling of anxiety's crept it's way into my brain.

"Here you go. And don't look now but you have an admirer." Darius drops a Corona in front of me and I lift my head to where he's pointing. A head of blonde hair and a serious stare is what I find.

Clara.

Delilah's good friend who let me in her house that night I took her out. She's eyeing me and my friends down as if unsure if she should come up to us or run away. There is a tall girl next to her with jet-black hair in a tight bun. She's whispering something into Clara's ear but it falls short because Clara steps forward in our direction.

"Hi." She stops in front of the tabletop and all three of us look at her.

"Hi Clara," I say, offering my hand. She shakes it wearily and keeps me in a locked stare. The girl that was with her steps up behind her and rests a hand on her shoulder.

"Babe, let's leave them alone. C'mon, I'll get you a drink." Her efforts are futile as Clara continues staring me down and suddenly I wished I was home once again. I'm not sure what Delilah told her or why she's looking at me like I killed her dog, but I don't think she likes me very much.

"If it isn't the infamous Mason Jones." She points to me haphazardly.

"Mhm, that'll be me. Nice to see you again." I'm not sure it was.

"Well," she nods and looks back at her girlfriend, I presume, before turning back to me. "Just be good to Delilah. Whatever it is between you two again, whatever your intentions are with being here. Just be good to her, okay?" Clara's brows furrow and I feel a sudden burst of respect at how protective she is of her friend.

"I don't want trouble." Darius and Shawn try not to laugh and I kick them under the table. "It's just nice to see her again. We're just friends." It was the truth. I didn't want to hurt her and I never would.

The word friends left a bitter taste in mouth. Sounded so futile in describe what she was to me.

"Good." She nods—but before she can say more my attention falls to the bar door, and as the bells ring my eyes catch a head of red hair. Delilah looks around before stopping on her friend and she makes her way over to the table, her friend and her girlfriend blocking her view from us.

This isn't happening.

"There you are, I've been texting you–" Delilah stops short. I watch as realization sets in that it's me and color rushes to her cheeks in a blush. Then she takes in my friends across the table, probably regretting coming out like myself.

"Hey Del." I raise my beer in her direction and flash her a smile. The blue on her cheeks grow and it's the cutest thing.

"Delilah, how good to finally meet you." Shawn stands and offers her his hand, I glare at him the entire time, the cheeky bastard smirking.

I'm sure both him and D were swimming in ideas of how to get more out of Del and how to push us together, which is why we need to leave as fast as possible.

"I'm Shawn, Mason's friend. We've heard so much about you." Fuck my life.

Delilah's face brightens and I watch her fight a smile. When her eyes meet mine again she smiles a real smile and I feel a sense of relief she didn't find it weird.

I'm going to kill Shawn.

"Here, there's plenty of room." Darius moves over and Shawn pulls up two chairs for Clara and her girl.

So this is how I ended up across my ex-girlfriend with my two best friends and her best friends at the other end of the table.

I should've stayed home.

"So, what brings you all out tonight." Shawn lifts his beer, reeling in my discomfort.

"Shawn likes to be outwardly annoying, feel free to ignore him. It's good to see you again Delilah." I watch Darius greet Del and wish that it was me who she was sitting next to and not my obnoxious best friend who was very married and definitely scheming.

"You too. How's the team?" I can't take my eyes off her as she talks at the table. She's wearing a cream sweater and from what I saw when she walked in black skinny jeans. Her curves hugged the black fabric making it look like it was made for her.

She made everything look like it was made for her.

Her full lips were tainted red and I couldn't help but wonder if she came from another bad date or was heading out on one. Then I reminded myself I had no right to that knowledge or to feel any bit jealous.

She wasn't mine, not anymore. We weren't anything to each other besides friends.

"I'm running to the bathroom," I announce to no one in particular but I catch Del's eyes as I stand. She watches as I walk away and I wish I didn't wear a long sleeve, suddenly hot. Everything about this situation was making me lose my mind. I was supposed to be forgetting about my problems for the night, not walking right into them.

"Mason." Delilah's voice catches me before I make it to the bathroom.

"You okay?" She hugs her green jacket to her chest and my eyes fall to her chest, she crosses her arms drawing my attention to the low-cut sweater.

It suddenly was ten times hotter.

"Yea, yea." I offer her a smile.

"I'm sorry if Clara overstepped by coming over. We can leave." She says.

"Don't worry Del. You're always welcome." I don't mean for it to come out heavy but it does. Both of us are stuck on the words and the deeper meaning. Treading on a fine line between desperation and wishful thinking.

I step forward, watching for any indication she doesn't want me near but I don't find one. Once I'm close enough to where I can smell her perfume and see the freckles that coat her nose I stop. Both of us stare at one another and I memorize all the features of her face that have changed.

She was still that girl.

I reach forward, brushing my hand across her cheek. She doesn't move or say anything.

"You look beautiful." I'm not sure what I'm doing but my voice is barely above a whisper. Her breath catches in her throat and I squeeze my hand into a fist to avoid touching her again, once already out of line.

"Thank you." She smiles and steps back, clearing her throat. "I'll see you back at the table." I watch as she walks away again, wondering what the fuck I'm going to do, wondering how I'm going to get myself out of this mess without any strings attached.

It sure as hell would be my hardest game yet.

15 - Delilah

Thinking back to two hours ago when I got a text from Clara asking if I'd like to meet her for drinks, I should've ignored it. Because now I'm sitting across from my best friend and my ex-boyfriend's best friends on a casual Monday night.

Great.

"So Delilah, tell us about yourself." The one who asks is Shawn. He's got brown floppy hair and reminds me of every popular teenage heartthrob. A boyish smile spreads across his lips and hasn't left.

"That's a loaded question." I take a big gulp of the beer Clara had ordered for me.

I wasn't one to normally drink beer so to say, I preferred my rum and cokes, but tonight I figured I'd be throwing back more than one in order to get through whatever this was. I tried to signal to Clara the second I got back from checking on Mason that we should probably leave. She decided to pretend she didn't feel the toe of my shoe kicking her shin.

I hate her.

"Well, you got our boy here all frazzled. I'd pay big money to be friends with the one who throws Mason Jones off his game." Shawn sends me a wink and Darius rolls his eyes. I assume the two are polar opposites and just by sitting here for a short ten minutes, I can already tell they are.

Darius is quiet and keeps to himself. Reserved and always observing, whereas Shawn is like a bubbly golden retriever who's always tugging on a leash. He hasn't stopped talking since I sat down and by the way Darius has pinched his eyebrows and thumbed his forehead twice already, this is an everyday occurrence.

"I highly doubt that," I say.

Nothing takes Mason off his game. Even this shoulder injury which is on its way to healing, won't ever take him off his game. He's the most focused person I've ever met in my life. If anyone can get through an awkward few months running into an ex-lover, it's him.

"You're just as in denial as him. Perfect match." Before I can come up with a response Clara shoots her glass of pinot on the table and choked on a laugh. Ryan rubs her hand up and down her girlfriend's back in concern all while trying not to laugh herself.

So we're all laughing at my misery, fantastic.

I kick Clara under the table again, but this time harder. She winces and flips me off with a smirk. I know her well enough that If she got the chance she would one hundred percent scheme away with Shawn in the dark corner of a room somewhere.

"You know, since you are technically single–" Shawn slides over so that his chair taps mine and I can see the whites of his eyes. His cologne is rich and musky, but unfamiliar. "How about a date, me and you?" He winks at the end.

There's no way he's seriously hitting on me in front of Darius with his best friend, my ex, in the bathroom. This man is bold, very bold, and if I wasn't so turned off by the idea of dating anyone right now I'd almost be impressed.

"Listen, Shawn. I bet you're—" I'm cut off by a gruff voice.

"Shawn." Mason comes to a stop right between Shawn and me, forcing me to look up at him. He looks down at his friend who wears a smug and knowing smile before bringing his arm down on the table between us. I watch as Shawn and Mason have some sort of silent conversation and shoot a look at Clara who wears an amused expression.

"Come with me." Mason's eyes are still on Shawn but his words are directed to me. He's tense, even more so than before by the bathrooms. I look between the two before standing and grabbing my beer.

Mason finally looks my way, his face blank. Without saying anything he moves the palm of his hand along my back and directs us to the door of the bar. I chug the rest of my beer, figuring I'd need the liquid courage, and drop it in a trash can before I'm shuffled out the front door.

"You know he was just trying to mess with you." I tease, crossing my arms to my chest as the chill of the January air hits my thin scrubs. Mason's still all tense and bunched up muscle but he moves quickly to take his jacket off and drape it across my own shoulders. The warmth is an instant welcome.

"He's a shithead." Mason squares his shoulders and clears his throat. "I'm sorry if he said anything out of hand. He can be annoying." We're leaning on the brick building now, his eyes avoidant of mine.

I wonder if he knows the effect he still has on me. The way our bodies are inches apart but all I can focus on is the smell of his familiar cologne and the heat of his body. I pull his jacket tighter and force myself to focus.

"How long have you all been friends?" I ask.

"A few months after I joined the team. Darius was my first friend on the squad and then Shawn kind of bulldozed his way into our friendship." He laughs at whatever memory is playing in his head and then looks up at me.

I smile up at him, taking it in.

"He sounds like a fun friend. I will say I'm a little nervous leaving him and Clara in the same room without me there." Mason's lips quirk up in another small laugh and it makes my skin prick to goosebumps.

He's devastatingly handsome. Even after all these years I still can't believe someone like him was into someone like me. He's extremely down to earth, always worrying about others and has the face of a romance cover model.

It wasn't fair.

"I'm sure they're taking advantage of the situation." He takes another step forward and again we find ourselves just a breath apart.

"How's your arm?" A stupid thing to say but I have to say something instead of doing something stupid. We're too close, it's messing with my head and my feelings.

I find myself wanting to pretend, just pretend for one night that things didn't change. That we're the same two people we were four years ago.

"You don't look like you're worried about my arm Delilah." His eyes grow darker in the night light and his jaw is clenched. He reaches out his hand, fingers grazing my cheek.

I should back away, go back inside and keep things friendly. We should step back and talk about the weather or the fact Shawn is probably making a move on my friends in the bar. We should be doing anything but this.

Anything but leaning into each other's warmth.

His hand stops on the bend of my neck and shoulder, his open palm warm and gripping firmly. I watch as several different emotions cross his face at once, his eyes pained. I don't think, I don't let myself do anything but soak up this moment.

"Mason." I bring my own hand up and grip his forearm, watching as he tenses and then relaxes at my touch. I realize now that his feelings towards touch may have gotten worse so I drop my fingers and whisper sorry.

"No." He picks my hand back up and squeezes it tightly. "You touch me right. You always have." He shows me what he means by bringing the palm of my hand to his chest and pushing inward. I realize he means the pressure and the tight grip of my hand from earlier.

I step forward, careful of his bad shoulder, and press my palm firmly into his chest, moving it along the tops of his left shoulder. I watch his face for discomfort but all I see is lust and longing.

He looks at me like I'm the only person alive, and at this moment I feel like we're the last two people on planet earth.

"What are we doing Del." He leans forward and ever so slowly rests his forehead on mine. I can feel the small puff of air as he breathes and I swallow hard. Suddenly I don't need the jacket that's wrapped around my shoulder, his warmth, and the way he makes me feel enough to heat me back to health.

"We're standing outside." We're doing something we shouldn't.

He laughs and I can feel it in my bones. And then he's leaning back and stepping even closer so that our bodies touch. He wraps his good arm around my back and pulls me close. I can't breathe properly, my own hands still pressed firmly between us on his warm chest.

"What do you want?" His voice is just above a whisper and I realize he's giving me full control of the situation. I wish he wouldn't.

I don't know what I'm doing, I know this isn't a good idea but it feels like a great one. We agreed to stay just friends and leave things uncomplicated. What we're doing right now seems exactly like complicating things.

"Don't ask me that. Ask me what I should want." I look up at him.

"What should you want Delilah?" He's so warm and so fucking handsome. I'm losing my sense of responsibility with every deep breath of his I can feel against my chest.

"I should want you to move away. To step back and ask me about the weather. I should want us to go back inside and have a normal cordial conversation with our friends." My voice is strained and my heart is beating so fast I can feel it in my throat.

He groans as if in pain at my words and grips my back tighter. His eyes close and he leans his forehead against mine again, this time his mouth open, breathing heavily.

"Don't say shit like that Del," I lean forward so that our noses touch and we both gasp.

What am I doing? I can feel every ounce of control leaving my body.

"Why." I'm pushing us both head-first over the ledge here.

"Because just last week you were telling me we're just friends but what's running though my head right now is anything but friendly. Friends don't think about friends the way I think about you." Okay so now I can't breathe.

He sucks in another breath when I bring my hands to his neck and squeeze.

I lean in, he leans down. Our lips are so close I can feel the smooth skin of his own every time he breathes. I close my eyes and swallow hard.

"Say the words Del, and I'm yours." He's so fucking close. His lips brush mine as the words come through. He quickly turns us so that my back is flat against the wall and his left hand now grips my hip, never moving away from me, still a breath apart.

If I say the words there's no going back, there's no taking back what crashes and falls afterward. If I take this selfish moment, this one night to pretend, I'll only hurt myself watching him leave again. But none of that even matters at this moment because he's all here and all warmth just a breath away, and I've been missing him for four fucking years.

It all seems so right there's no way it could be wrong.

No one warns you about your real first heartbreak. Especially when it's one with no cheating or foul play. When it's all right at the wrong time, there's nothing that heals a wound of what could've been. Nothing answers to the pain, nothing except maybe this moment.

It's been years of trying to move on, trying to ignore the familiar sting his name would bring every time I saw it on TV. Years pretending like I had found a way to live with the ache, but it was all a bluff.

I think I've finally found my own brand of novocaine, and I'm willing to bet my heart to get some.

"Kiss me," I say, sealing my fate.

I hear him breathe out a small– thank god, before his lips come crashing down on my own. I almost faint the second they do, the feeling so familiar yet brand new. He tugs me close and moves his head at an angle to kiss me deeper and I grip his shirt to stay standing.

I pretend that we're strangers falling in love again just for this moment, this one fleeting moment.

16 - Delilah

Warmth.

I'm so warm, everything about this moment radiates heat. The warm breath of air he lets out between the connection of our lips. The heat of his body pushed up against mine.

We're each other's warmth in the frigid January air. We're standing outside of the local bar full of people who will gossip, tell their friends, and maybe even the media. But none of it matters, because for now, we're pretending.

Although this kiss feels wholeheartedly real.

He squeezes my hip like I'm slipping away, but I'm nothing but permanent against him. His chest and mine move heavily against one another. Running my hands along his shoulders, careful of his right, I soak in the feel of him.

Our mouths fight for dominance, like each of us, can't get enough. He drops his head to the bend of my neck and I squint my eyes shut the second his teeth graze a vein.

"Fuck," I'm breathless.

He comes back up, eyes heavy and barely open. Both of us breathe heavily ready for whatever comes next. I lean in to press our lips together again and he meets me halfway.

His hand on my hip slides to rest on the exposed skin of my risen scrub top. The feeling makes me weak in the knees, every part of my senses shot.

"Del girl, you're killing me." He groans into my mouth, teeth biting my bottom lip gently. He pulls back and presses my hands firmly to his chest.

For a moment I forget where we are, what we're doing, and who we are. I forget that we're in public, pressed against the wall of a bar. I forget that he's Mason Jones, THE quarterback and that we're supposed to be friends.

But the moment is over almost as quick as it comes.

Clara bursts through the door on our right and I push Mason back, swiping my arm across my lips. Mason coughs, adjusting himself before turning away.

"There you are! We thought he kidnapped you or something!" She's smiling knowingly and I dread the conversation I'm about to get on the way home.

"We were just talking." I almost laugh at the lie that leaves my lips. Masons short wavy hair is a mess and I look like I just ran a half mile.

She gives me a deadpan look and rolls her eyes.

"Mhm. Anyways, I'm tired and hungry. You ready to go?" She points to Ryan who's holding the car keys, always our designated driver as she doesn't drink more than one, or if that.

I nod my head yes and hold out my finger as if to say one minute. She turns on her heels and follows Ryan to the corner of the street where they parked.

The silence grows between the two of us, reality like an ice pack to a burn.

"We'll, I'm gonna—" I pointed to the car, not knowing what to say. He turns back to face me, face unreadable. He's probably regretting every moment that led us here, wishing he didn't come out tonight.

I'd like to say I am too, but I can't lie to myself.

That felt good. But that's all it can ever do for me, one fleeting moment.

"Okay." He clears his throat and furrows his eyebrows. For a moment I think he's going to say more but he doesn't. He steps forward, reaching out to brush his hand along my face one more time, and then heads back into the bar.

I've been outside this entire time but for the first time since stepping out, I breathe.

By the time I make it to the car Clara and Ryan are on their phones listening to music, waiting. They both look up when I climb in the back seat.

"Don't say anything." I point to Clara who wears a smirk.

"I'm not. But you've got some lip gloss right here," she points to the corner of my lip and I swat her hand away.

Tonight was a mistake, I shouldn't have let myself go like that. I am older, and more responsible now. I had plans and a life, all without him in them.

Making out with my ex was not part of the plan, and shouldn't be.

"It was just a kiss. That's all." Even I don't convince myself as I try and convince them. Clara looks at me through the rearview with a smirk.

"It's never just a kiss Delilah. Especially with him. What happened?" The car is dead silent and I can practically hear the curiosity seeping out of their ears.

"It just, like, happened. I don't know. One moment we were just talking about Shawn teasing him and then my brain got all blurry." I huff.

They both look at one another and then burst out laughing, making me want to curl up and disappear. Of course, they'd find my love life amusing.

"Oh, Delilah. You're totally going down." Ryan says, turning up the music.

I flip them both off.

They're right in a way. If I continue to let myself break my own barriers around him there's no stopping me from falling again. And I can't, not right now. Not when I'm so close to graduating and possibly moving.

My career is my focus and I already have all those who I love around me.

There is no room for any ex-boyfriend quarterbacks.

~~~

I come home to an emotional wreck of a father on the couch watching old home videos of mom. It was actually my mom's idea to get the old VHS tapes transferred onto a hard drive, something she loved to watch with all of us.

He's sitting on the couch when I walk in, beer in hand and half-open eyes. His favorite video is playing on the screen, one of me and mom on Easter looking for Easter eggs.

I try to slip away as quietly as possible, not wanting to disturb him or get involved. I found it best to ignore him when he was in this state, otherwise, I'd just anger him and make matters worse.

I manage to make it to my room without him lifting his head, and locking the door. I slip out of my jacket and shoes, dropping my purse to the chair that's tacked high with clothes I've yet to fold.

Between going to work, studying for hours and trying to avoid Mason, and doing terribly, I've had almost zero time to do anything important. Like self-care.

I take a long hot shower, change into my pajamas and climb into bed.

My phone buzzes on my nightstand and I instantly panic as I read the message that's lighting up my room.

Mason: I'm sorry.

What's he sorry for? Does he regret it? Oh god, he regrets it, he regrets it real bad. I knew I should've kept things friendly but I know I couldn't have been alone at that moment.

I know he felt it too. It was impossible not to, palpable even.

Me: It's fine. Lapse in judgment.

Mason: I'm not sorry for kissing you Del. I'm sorry for not doing it sooner.

I think I've lost count of how many times my heart has felt like it stopped tonight. First was the second I saw him, and most memorable was the second his lips touched mine.

What am I doing?

I hover over the empty message bubble trying to come up with a logical response because clearly all logic has been tossed out the window tonight. There was something so freeing about just letting it all go.

I turn my phone off instead of replying and head out to the kitchen to get water and delaying my response.

"Delilah? That you?" Dad's voice cracks through the silence. I step out of the kitchen and answer.

"Yep, just me Dad."

I step into the living room trying my best to avoid the video on the tv, just another painful reminder of what I've lost tonight.

"You make dinner?" His words are slurred and the beer that's on the table next to him is half empty. I wonder just how many he's gone through tonight.

"It's late, I got dinner after I left work." I point to the time below the tv.

He's usually never this bad and it worries me that he's drinking tonight. I thought his therapy had been going well, and he was slowly dealing with it. But I guess even the worst days still make their way through.

"You should get to bed, I can make your favorite dinner tomorrow." I step in front of the tv and grab his half-empty beer. He groans a nonanswer and I ignore him.

If he wants to sleep on the couch all night then so be it.

I recycle his can, noting the several others in the bin, and make my way back into my room. By the time I climb under the covers, I've completely forgotten about the text message I'd left unanswered.

It's times like these I wish I had my mom here. She'd know what to say and what to do. I'm sure she'd be absolutely devastated at how Dad's handling it all and I wish more than anything I could take all his pain away.

I try to imagine if things went differently, imagine if she was still here, laughing in the living room with him right now watching those old videos.

Fuck this hurts.

I grip my chest and can't help the tears that fall.

Tonight was the night to let it all go and just feel. Tomorrow was set back to reality.

17 - Mason

"How's the shoulder?"

My dad takes a bite of his steak without looking up from his plate. He and Marie have been back for a week now, both of them making living here impossibly awkward. Dad has made it abundantly clear he doesn't want me here and Marie overcompensating for Dad's cold shoulder.

"Fine."

The doctor says everything is looking good. Still can't move to any movement whatsoever and it's making my skin crawl. I've read the fantasy book Del dropped off at my house and even ordered another on Amazon.

Never thought I'd say that.

"When can you throw again?" He looks up this time, glaring at me from across the table. I hope he gets permanent wrinkles from the constant unbearing mood he's always in.

"I don't know Dad. Never." I joke, forking a piece of lettuce.

"Don't say shit like that Mason. You need to throw again." He shakes his head and I nod mine.

Riveting conversation, will think about it years from now. But it's true, it feels like I'll never throw a ball again and will spend the rest of my life reading books and withering away in this shell of a house.

Dinner proceeds silently and I'm thankful for it. I think about the team and how they're doing just fine without me. They've made it to the playoffs and are in good standing to make it to the big game. It kills me to not be a part of it but the second I'm cleared for more than just sitting around I'll be there for them.

I have a meeting with Coach and the trainers tonight at 5 to discuss my recovery with the team. I'm dreading that talk and looking Coach in the face again in weeks. I know he can't help but be disappointed in losing his QB weeks before the playoffs, I know I am.

I help Marie with the clean up and curse the deadbeat I call Dad as he leaves his plate and takes off to his office.

As strained as my relationship with my own parents are, Marie has been nothing but nice to me. She's always made her best effort to be there and bridge the gap between us even if that bridge crumbles every time.

"Listen, Mason, I know your father isn't the best at expressing his concern, but he is worried about you." Marie passes me a plate and I pay it dry with my one good arm.

"It's fine Marie. You don't have to attempt to make it up for him. He's a grown man and can tell me himself." Even though he'd never do that. Showing me he cares would be like pulling a tooth.

"We'll, you're right of course. Just know we're here for you. I am if you ever need anything." She smiles and it's warm and welcoming as it always is.

Sometimes I find myself thinking about my own mom when she looks at me. If she had made different choices than the ones that led her to where she is. If she found peace in me and Dad instead of drugs.

What "ifs" lead you down a drain that never clears.

"Thank you, I appreciate it." I offer her a smile and finish off the dishes. By the time we're done, it's close to meeting time so I set up my laptop in my room, being sure to close the door.

I've been checking my phone like a loser since the kiss.

Maybe telling Delilah I should've kissed her sooner was a push, but it wasn't a lie. I'm not going to lie to myself or her, she's always been special to me. She's always been a part of me that I'm proud of.

Seeing her again has cracked open my closed heart. I'm determined to make her see that we can have fun and be the people we are today. Maybe our story isn't finished yet.

At least I'd try.

But for now, I need to face the story of my career so I shut off my phone and focus on not overthinking for the next hour.

~~~

That was the hardest call of my life.

My beer tastes like a bandaid on a gaping wound that the call carved opened. They all sounded guarded and the way they talked was as if my future with the team was uncertain.

Un–fucking–certain.

Like shoulder surgery at the start of my career was too much of a risk for the team to take. That own thought had my brain exploding more than the migraine I'd have tomorrow after all this drinking.

I was young, I'd recover from this. It's like they don't believe in me. The player who helped bring the team to a Super Bowl within my first year.

I wasn't a failure.

So why did I feel like it?

The only good thing about my dad's wealth and this empty house was the back porch. All glass and heated, it made sitting outside but inside during the winter—enjoyable.

It's also where I kept my own stash of beer and allowed myself to soak up all the self-pity. I couldn't work out, I couldn't throw, I couldn't play. I couldn't do any of my normal de-stressors so I've resorted to the worse.

Drinking.

It felt good to feel nothing. At this moment the trees outside are covered in several inches of snow, and the ground is covered in ice from the storm that happened last night.

My phone rings from the floor and I turn, wincing as my shoulder throbs, and pick it up. I toss the beer can to the floor and answer it.

"Hello?" My voice is hoarse from not talking and trying not to cry like a fucking loser.

"Mason." Her voice shoots a laser down my spine and I sit up.

"Delilah, hey." Fuck, I should've checked the caller ID, I wouldn't have answered right now like this.

"Hey. I just thought I'd call and check-in." She pauses. "With your shoulder. You know, your recovery?." She sounds nervous and I'd kill to see her cheeks warm up like I know they are.

I wish she wasn't asking about my recovery. I wish she was asking about that kiss, but she was always good at deflecting and focusing on what matters most.

"It's fine, just fine." I laugh internally at how much of a loser I must look like right now, laying on a couch surrounded by beer cans and thinking about all my life choices.

And talking to my ex.

"You don't sound fine." She reads me like a script.

Another thing she was always good at. "Well, broken shoulder and unsure career, not much to be happy about at the moment." I pinch nose in concentration.

She takes a deep breath and I know she's about to say something to try and make me feel better. In reality, she may be the only one who could, but not like this, not over the phone and complaining.

"Mason. Don't say that. You'll recover and be back on the team in no time. Give your body some credit." She says.

"Mhm, will do." I sigh and lean back. "I'll call you another day Del, now's not the best time." I don't want to put all my shitty thoughts on her. She deserves all of me, not broken me.

"Don't do that. Don't push someone away who's trying to help." Her voice is stern. "Do you want me to come over there?" She speaks quietly as if whispering into the phone.

Do I want her to come over? And see me like this? No. Do I want her? Have I wanted her? Always.

"Delilah, you know I'd never complain if you showed up on my doorstep, but I'm not okay right now." I clench my teeth at the admission. "I just want to be alone." Control was slipping through my fingertips.

"Alright. Be safe Mason. And just now that you've got people that are there for you. That will always be there." I wish she was still here, I wish we were still us.

"Do you remember," I cleared my throat. "That time I sprained my ankle at practice and I thought my life was over." I laugh, blinking back pity tears. I blame my drunken state for all the heightened emotion. "And how, you called me a crybaby and played nurse all night. I think it was after that you decided you were going to be a PA to fix all my football wounds." The memory was as clear as looking through glass.

I grab onto it rather than letting it go. I sink into it rather than sink into my reality.

"I do." She laughs softly. "And that was a joke. I wanted to be a PA long before you buddy." I can practically hear her smile through the phone.

It's silent for several breaths, both of us reliving that moment, maybe even more. I wonder if she thinks about times before? I wonder if they carry into her dreams as they do mine.

"I miss you so goddamn much Del," I whisper, revealing what my mind has always kept locked away. "I miss us." I hear an intake of breath but don't regret saying it.

It's been years—yet coming home has been nothing but a reminder of what could have been.

"Don't do this tonight Mason. You're hurting, I get that, we have happy memories together that help you at your lowest. I cherish that for you." She takes a breath. "But don't start something we both know we can't finish. Focus on you, focus on your recovery, it's what's best." She was right. I know she's right, but it doesn't sound right.

What if we could finish it this time? What if we could cross that line, what if we could be what we always wanted?

I'm never drinking again.

"I'm sorry. You're right. I gotta go," I cough.

"Wait, Mas—" I hung up, not wanting to hear her feel bad for me. I'll apologize tomorrow and we'll go back to being just friends. I'll remember as little of this day as possible.

And I'll work like hell to recover.

18 - Delilah (before)

Four Years Ago

"Mason, you need to get off of me."

I shove the solid mass that is my half-asleep snoring boyfriend. I know he has a practice in an hour and will kick himself in the shin for not being up by now. I can hardly breathe under him and the added morning weightlifting is doing nothing to help my cause.

Well, it may be. Considering I get to look at this man naked on a daily.

He groans loudly, rolling over and throwing an arm up over his head. He's taking up every inch of the bed and he's still a morning grump. I usually fight a nightly battle with both the covers and trying to breathe under him.

Mason Jones is a severe cuddler in his sleep.

"Ten more minutes," his voice is deep and scratched like it always is in the morning. I shake my head and roll to the side, throwing the warm cocoon of covers off my body. Wearing nothing but Mason's t-shirt I go to stand, but get nowhere because his arm shoots out around my waist, pulling me back to bed.

"MASON!" I screech at the feeling of being lifted and then dropped onto a hard body. I turn, straddling his hips and sitting back on his stomach. His eyes are still closed but his mouth is turned up into a teasing smile and his hands crawl up my sides.

Looking at him in the morning light, in our bed in our very own apartment makes me a little queasy. I can't believe this boy I knew from high school who everyone loved would give me a chance. The boy with rich parents and a parade of admirers following him wherever he goes would set his heart on mine.

"I can feel you staring." He grumbles, squeezing my sides and causing a laugh to fall through my lips. He knows how ticklish I am there.

"Good," I say.

In about ten minutes he's going to get up panicked and talk to himself the entire time he gets ready, going on and on about how he needs to stop sleeping in. He'll know not to complain to me because I already did my duty in trying to wake him up.

Instead, he'll give me puppy eyes and a kiss goodbye all while cursing himself.

His hands move down my exposed legs and suddenly I'm hyper-aware of the lack of underwear I'm wearing and the lack of shirt his chest bares. We're skin to skin and If I don't get out of here, we won't for the next hour.

He was irresistible and we couldn't get enough of one another.

"Babe," I whisper.

He doesn't respond but does open his eyes, and the only warning I get before he's pushing me back playfully onto his groin is a wink and smirk. I slap his chest the second my bare self touches his strained boxers. He's hard and most definitely ready for me, and I can't say I'm too far behind him.

"You're gonna be late," I wiggle my hips over his growing erection, leaning down we both moan into each other's mouths. He throws his head back and releases my hips and I stop moving over him. I pepper kisses on his neck and cheek, avoiding his mouth for the sake of morning breath.

"Later," I whisper into his ear and scrape my teeth along his jaw.

He loves when I'm rough with my kisses, loves when I leave a mark on his neck or his chest, even on his hip. I'm sure his teammates give him shit in the locker room but he never complains, and always says he loves the reminder of me on him.

I give him one more peck on the nose and slide off of him, hearing him groan in the process. He watches me stand and his eyes drift down my legs and linger on where the old gray t-shirt cuts off just before mid-thigh.

"Mason. Get up, you have practice in–" I turn, looking at the nearest clock. "Twenty minutes now." His eyes widen and he shoots out of bed, pillows, and blankets flopping to the floor. I laugh as he stumbled into the en suite bathroom already pulling down his boxer briefs and giving me a grateful glimpse of his perfect ass.

Why do men always have perfect butts? I swear, I've always had wide thighs but lacked the meat on my backside. Mason swears he loves my butt, the perfect amount to grab and cuddle, but he's biased. He's always horny.

"Fuck, fuck." I hear swearing coming from the bathroom, shower now going. I make my way into the kitchen, feeding our pet fish Hershey named after Mason's favorite chocolate bar who we spent way too long getting the proper tank size and enrichment for, before making myself and the late football player a cup of coffee.

I have finals coming up and plan to spend my time at the library after classes today because it's the only place I could really focus. Between the clingy horny boyfriend and my lack of staying on task, I barely could do shit around here.

But I loved it.

"Shit, I'm so fucking annoyed. I always do this." Mason stumbles into the kitchen, hair wet and chest bare. He's wearing a pair of athletic shorts and is hopping on one foot to pull on his sneakers. I watch, sipping my coffee against the counter, as water slips down every dip of ab muscle on his perfect body.

Maybe being late wouldn't be so bad.

He finally gets his sneakers on and steps up to where I'm leaning against the counter. I look up at him, handing the tumbler of coffee I made him with a smile.

"You always do this, and then proceed to not set your alarm any earlier. Or pull me back into bed, every time." I wink, sipping my coffee.

He shakes his head and takes the tumbler.

"When you have the most beautiful girl by your side, or on top of you, in nothing but your own t-shirt. Getting out of bed seems like climbing Mt. Everest." His eyes light up as he talks and I can't help the way my heart skips a beat.

Over a year into this relationship and he still makes me feel like he did in the first month. I never want that to change, I never want us to change. We work so well, both of us prioritizing ourselves and one another. We both have goals and ambitions yet make the time for what matters most to us right now.

I hope we never lose sight of that.

"I love you," he leans in, wrapping a heavy arm around my waist and pulling me close. His lips descend on mine and I close my own, giving him a walled kiss and shaking my head. He pulls back and pinches my ass.

"OW!" I swat at his chest and he catches my arm tugging me even closer. "No kisses before I brush my teeth, which occurs after I have my coffee." I say under my breath.

"I don't care Delilah. I've heard you fart in your sleep and eat you out on a nightly basis. A little morning breath won't hurt." My cheeks feel warm and I mentally curse him for always having to bring up something sexual. And what does that have to do with breath?

Vagina and breath? Is he okay? I sometimes wonder what goes on his head to come up with the responses he does. I really do wonder how many brain cells are working away in there. However many there, he's still the love of my life.

He leans in again and this time I give in, bringing my own arms around his shoulders and raising on my toes. He kisses me as if he'll never kiss me again and goosebumps shoot up my spine. His fingers grip my ass again and I feel a shot of pleasure go down south.

He pulls back, pecks my lips once more, and smiles.

"Gotta go, please be wearing this exact outfit later. I haven't stopped thinking about bending you over the bed fucking you until we both come at least twice." He says it casually like he's reading off the morning news, and I almost choke on my spit.

"Love you too," I say still in shock at his crude words.

He slaps my ass once more for good measure and then he's out the door. Locking it behind him I run my hands over my face.

Great, now I need at least thirty minutes of alone time with myself and my forever-reliable vibrator. I drop my coffee cup, now empty, into the sink and run for my bedroom. Finding my purple friend, I flop onto the bed.

Just as I'm about to turn it on I think of "getting even" payback for turning me on before he leaves for practice. I'll show him what he missed this morning and make him suffer through practice with a hard on. Perfect.

Grabbing my phone I take a picture of the vibrator and smile as I hit send. The little "read" message pops up immediately and what follows is a reply.

19 - Delilah

Present

"SHIT" I jumped out of bed covered in sweat, heart racing.

For a moment I forget where I am and what year it is. The dream felt so real and so natural, which in a way it was. After talking to Mason on the phone last night and worrying more than I should have, I dreamt of that same memory.

It was after that practice he sprained his ankle, it was that night he came home, and instead of the salacious plans he had for us, I helped him get out in bed and ice it. I rub at my chest from the stinging that memory brings.

We were so good.

I'm losing sight of time now. I'm mixing memories and reality and forcing my heart to do all the deciphering, which can only lead to my own demise.

"Fuck," I sigh.

Reaching for my phone I note the time and how I have an hour before I'm meeting my Dad for lunch in town. I was supposed to meet Tish but she got called into work for something last minute so instead, I invited my dad. I figured we could use the time to really talk.

After the night of drinking, I was worried about him, more than usual. I wondered if he was skipping his therapy appointments, or if it wasn't working anymore. But what really worries me is that he's fallen back to the beginning of his grief where he wasn't near a stage of being ready for therapy. If that's the case, going won't change anything.

Deciding I should get the day started, I spend thirty minutes showering and getting ready. My phone buzzes just as I'm starting my car.

Clara: Did you see this?

-image attachment

Opening the image my heart sinks. It's a news article from a local station highlighting Mason's return, but it's not the fact they're covering Mason that causes my stomach to twist. It's the image and headline.

Mason Jones heads home for recovery; could a new girl be his medicine?

Below the sad excuse for a headline is a picture of us both inside Old Joe's. We're not touching but we're looking at one another like more than strangers. Someone must've taken it when I went to check on him after my friends showed up unexpectedly.

Okay, so it's not the worst thing that could've happened. I guess this should be expected considering he's a public figure and this town is not ALL locals. Besides, it could've been a picture of us kissing and that would've been an absolute meltdown. I'm sure I'd get calls from every relative I've ever had.

And I'm sure Mason's team wouldn't like it.

Is even being pictured with me and this daunting headline bad exposure? And now suddenly I'm worrying about him looking bad because he's at a bar with friends when he should be at home and laying low.

What exactly was on my bingo card for this year? Did I pick the wildest card known to man?

Deciding to forget about the text I ignore Clara and turn off my phone to make the short drive into town for some lunch with Dad.

—-

"I just want to start out with an apology, which I know you're tired of, Hun." My Dad sighs, laying his napkin out on his lap. I watch as he clears his throat and avoids eye contact, clear signs of his guilt and unease.

I had to give it to him for admitting an apology right away, clearly, he had been thinking about it.

"I shouldn't be drinking like that, especially around you. I shouldn't be putting that weight on your shoulders." I nod as he speaks, picking up my chopsticks to dig into my Paitan ramen.

Totto Ramen has been a staple for me throughout finishing school, I think I come here at least three times a month, I'm obsessed.

"And I want you to know that from now on I'm going to be taking my mental health more seriously, I'm going to tell my therapist about how I haven't been doing good and we're going to come up with a plan." He looks up at me and I swallow back tears.

It's one thing watching a parent die. It's another watching one become a shell of who they used to be. Watching them go off the rails and become less of a pillar in your life and more of a responsibility. It was strange, in a way, to feel like you become the parent at times. Like when he's too drunk to walk and I help him to bed, the same way he did when I learned to take my first steps. Or how you watch someone so mentally fortified just...break.

Parents are people too, but nothing prepares you as a child to grow up and watch the reality sink in.

"I'm glad Dad. I want us to move forward, and most importantly I want you to be okay. Not only for me but especially for you." I reach my hand out, taking his. "We're a team. We've gotten through the worst, we can get through the aftermath." I smile, wiping a tear that reluctantly fell.

"Now eat your Ramen so it doesn't get cold." I joke, clearing my throat to ignore the heaviness in my chest.

We were best at this, being silent. It wasn't a bad thing or a good one. It was a new normal of sorts, one that keeps us on our feet. I have hope that with time, even though it feels as though all we've had is time, we'll get back to a steady relationship.

I know how hard it is to battle with yourself, mentally, it can be one you lose. I'm just glad he's here with me now and willing to talk to me openly.

"So have you seen Mason lately?" My dad looks up at me with a sly smile.

"Why are you smiling at me like that?" I shake my head and take a bite of ramen. "There is nothing going on so don't look at me like that. He and I are just friends." I say, swallowing my food.

I can feel the heat rise to my cheeks so I take a sip of water.

I look around the restaurant and note that there isn't anyone here I know, hoping I can smooth past these conversations as quickly as possible without the entire town of Portsneck knowing my dad was discussing Mason Jones.

"Yea, okay Del." He laughs at my obvious embarrassment.

Why does everyone have zero trust in me? I can handle him being back, I can handle the fact I kissed him again. I can handle wet dreams about him while the possibility of running into him at work, in town, and anywhere looms over my head like a dark cloud.

I can handle it.

"Everyone has zero hope in me. It's kind of insulting." I fake indifference.

"Delilah. He was the love of your life. You both worshiped the ground each of you walked on. Anyone who knew you could feel your love from miles away." He takes a sip of water. "If your mom was here she'd tell you the same. You loved that boy, even still might." He manages to mention mom without flinching and I'd be more focused on that if it wasn't for the fact he not so subtly hinted that I was still in love with Mason.

I was not.

We were not in love anymore. I've gotten over him, he's gotten over me. The recent kiss was just a lapse in judgment.

"I don't love him, dad. Not anymore." I told him.

He wipes his mouth with a napkin and shakes his head.

"All I'll say is, it's not very often you get second chances in life." His eyes drop in sadness, and my stomach turns as I think of mom. "So if it's anything coming from your old man, take them while you can." He finds my hand across the table and squeezes it.

I know he's trying to say if he had a second chance at a full life with mom he'd jump on it in a heartbeat—we both would. But that was different, that was sickness. This was juvenile love and heartbreak. Mason being back in town was not a sign of a second chance at us, but rather a sign of my past reminding me of why I'm here doing what I love.

We both finish eating in peace and pay the bill shortly after. I drive us both home and stop to get ice cream on the way, and Lactaid pills because my digestive system repels my love for ice cream. Dad is quiet for the drive but I feel good about him for the first time in a while. We managed to briefly talk about mom at dinner and he even attempted relationship advice.

That's what I like to call good ol' trying.

"Del, I love you, hun. Thank you for dinner and for listening to me. I'm here for you always, even when It seems like I'm off somewhere else. You are, and will always be my baby girl." I've just turned the corner into the hallway where he stands. My dad pulls me into a hug and this time I let the tears fall.

I've missed him, and I will continue to miss him as he gets better. But holding him, the fact he's here, is all I need.

"Love you too, Dad. I need you but I want you to be happy again." I pull away. "You're gonna get through this." I squeeze his hands before letting them go. He gives me a kiss on my forehead like he's done since I was a little girl and wishes me goodnight.

For the first time in a while, I went to bed content and happy. Happy about dinner and having our talk. Happy about having a good group of friends who I love, and happy that in a weird way Mason being back in town has brought up old wounds I may finally be ready to heal.

20 - Mason

"You're looking really good Mason. I'm very impressed with your progress." Doctor Karr took a step back from where she was feeling my right shoulder. Another week of rest and waiting is finally paying off.

It's been a few weeks now since the surgery and every day I feel myself getting stronger and stronger. My arm becomes less of a worry as the pain subsides. I can see the finish line but it's still unfortunately unattainable.

At least for a while.

"I'd say by our next visit we can take off that sling and set you up with a physical therapist to get you to minimal movement. It's still a long road ahead but you're done a good job so far with keeping it steady and allowing it to heal. All of which leads to throwing sooner." She smiles while getting her things together.

"Thank you. I can't wait for the next appointment." Just the thought of being able to remove the sling for more than just the appointments has my head spinning. I can't fucking wait to be rid of it.

Checking out afterward is a blur and I immediately call Darius to give him the news. He's been busy with playoffs, and the team progressing even further.

They've just secured the AFC east championship title and are on their way to securing the entire AFC. The team is solid and no matter how hard it is to admit it, they're doing just fine without me.

Dr. Callahan called me yesterday, the team's specialty doctor, to catch up on my prognosis and how I was doing. He sounded just as pleased with my progress as Dr. Karr and says he hopes to see me back in Boston soon.

Theoretically, once the sling is off plus another week of healing, I could go back up to my apartment in Boston. Considering I've done all my initial recovery and the team will want to work out my physical therapy, there would be no real reason to stay here for the rest of it.

At least not one I've come to accept yet.

When I got home it was just Marie who I hear bustling around, assuming Dad was still upstairs working. He rarely leaves his office during the day and his car was in the driveway telling me he is still there.

I shower and change into something comfortable before heading downstairs for another mind numbing dinner with decent food and lack of conversation.

When I get down there I'm surprised to see just Marie sitting at the dining room table, a room vacant beside her. I can tell immediately something is off.

She wipes her cheeks and looks up at me with tears in her eyes.

"What's wrong, what's happened?" I step into the room, feeling suffocated with worry. I rarely see her cry, which makes me nervous as is.

She smiles sadly at me, wiping her eyes with a tissue.

"Nothing Mason, don't worry about me. Your dad and I just had a small argument is all. I'll get started on dinner." She stands, looking like she's about to break.

"What the fuck did he say to you." I clench my fist and look her in the eye. "Did he hurt you?" Just the thought makes me sick to my stomach but I've seen my dad angry and although he's never laid a hand on me, I wouldn't put it past him.

"Oh god no, no no Mason." She shuffles over to me. "It's nothing, we just had a little disagreement. You sit down and I'll get things ready." Before I can pry her for more information she leaves, sniffling in the process.

Absolutely not. My pathetic excuse for a father can shit on me all he wants, but not Marie. Marie and I may not have the best relationship but she was a sweetheart, always looking out for me even when I'm unapproachable.

I storm upstairs, taking them two at a time hoping Marie stays in the kitchen so she doesn't have to hear us fight. I make my way down the empty hallway, no pictures of us, no indication that there is a family who even lives there.

Fitting.

I bang my fist on the door of my dad's office, waiting to hear from him.

"Jesus, relax." He whips the door open and we meet eye to eye.

I'm at least an inch taller than him but he holds his own on me. We both are cut from the same string, too stubborn to admit our faults, and too damn emotional with no control over how to handle them. At Least I can admit when I have a problem, and I've gotten the help I need.

He's kept it to himself for years and will continue to do so.

"Why the fuck are you making Marie cry." I clench my jaw, hating the way he looks at me like I'm a bother.

"What I talk to my wife about is none of your concern, now go downstairs." He moves to close the door but I stick my leg out instead, shoving my way through.

"No, you listen to me. I've been home for almost a month and you've treated me like shit. I'm used to that, but what I'm not used to is seeing Marie cry. So what the fuck did you do?" He steps up to me and throws a finger in my face.

"Don't you raise your voice at me, Mason?" He sits and I swear I see red.

I just stare back at him, waiting for him to admit what's got him worse than usual lately. He's sometimes tolerable, sometimes not. But the last week has been suffocating with his mood swings and now Marie is in the kitchen crying over a disagreement?

"Just tell me what's going on." I stand my ground, watching him as he moves to take a seat behind his desk. He shakes his head, reaching for a pen and paper. He doesn't answer me at first, and for a moment I think he's just going to ignore me.

I watch as he carefully writes something on the paper, his face stoic and jaw clenched like whatever he's writing is bothering him.

"Your mom called. For more money." He caps the pen and tosses it on the desk. He stands and I tense. "Here's the fucking address she asked to send it to. So you want to be all Mr. Tough guy! Here. Take this address, take this responsibility." The paper is shoved into my chest and I grab it from his hand.

"It's your problem now." He turns and I look down at the paper.

It's an address for somewhere up in New Hampshire. Scribbled on top is the amount of money I presume she wants.

Money. That's what she wants. Not me, not to check up on her only son. Not to see if I'm doing okay with recovery, or to see how I am with my career. No, she wants money.

Drug money.

"This still doesn't explain why Marie was crying." My voice is strained, and my brain feels fuzzy. I don't look up from the paper.

"Marie thinks I should try and get her help again. She thinks I should go see her and try. I simply told her that was not happening again. Not again." I crumpled the paper up and shoved it in my jeans pocket.

My mother for as long as I remember has struggled with drug addiction. It started after I was born, with postpartum depression. Everyone says she was never the same after me, that she changed drastically. No amount of therapy or both inpatient and outpatient programs helped her.

Addiction was a disease, and it was one she could not win against.

"You didn't have to make her upset. You didn't have to raise your voice at her." I say.

He looks up at me, tired and unforgiving. Except for this time, his eyes show the years of sadness he spent mourning the loss of his marriage to the mother of his son. The person he fell in love with, is now someone unrecognizable.

I lost a mother I never really knew. A mother who gave birth to me, and then could never recover from the depression of it.

"You're right. And I'll apologize to her." That's all he gives me but I'll take it.

We'll never be the loving father and son duo and I'm perfectly okay with that. My father and I had never gotten along great, and I'm sure even if my mother had never fallen into addiction, we'd still be the same.

I leave his office, not wanting to talk to him anymore. I make sure to stop in the kitchen and tell Marie I'm sorry and that he is too. She just gives me a hug, to which I tense, but pat her back anyway. I tell her I'm going to head out for dinner instead so she doesn't have to worry about cooking.

Also, give her and dad time to talk.

Give him time to apologize.

It's only around six thirty so plenty of places are still open. I don't want to go alone and I really only have one friend here that I'd want to go with.

A friend who I don't want to be just a friend.

Me: Want to meet for dinner?

It's been a few days since our conversation while I was drunk. I texted her the next day apologizing for hanging up as I did, but that was the end of it. I haven't heard from her since and I have a feeling it will be like that unless I'm the one who reaches out.

I've played this game before, I'll play it again if I have to.

Del: Sure, but I'm studying for an exam. Want to come by and we can order takeout?

For someone who just wants to stay my friend and forget about our past or the kiss, she sure is trying to get me alone. First, her wanting to come by and check on me the other day and now asking me over?

I'm not sure I'm the one confused about the line drawn.

What I do know is that I'll take what I can get. I know that there is a part of me, deep down, that is afraid to admit what I've been feeling. Afraid to confront what I think I know since being back here.

Since being back in this town, back in her life. I've had no desire to check my messages from girls in Boston. Or to check my Instagram DMs for who's trying to slide in while I'm injured. Three months ago I would've been all for it, living for the attention.

I've spent years forgetting what it was like to belong to someone and it's only taken one girl, a deep past, and four weeks to remind me how good belonging feels. It's taken a bright smile, red hair and a big heart to remind me of what I've missed out on. What I've spent the last four years trying to fill.

And that scared the hell out of me.

21 - Delilah

If I look at another line in this textbook I think my brain is going to explode. I've been studying nonstop since the moment I woke up, and my stomach is caving in. When Mason texted all I saw was an opportunity for food.

And maybe to see him.

A part of me has been missing him, and missing Mason is a dangerous thing considering he doesn't even permanently live here anymore. Danger can also be exhilarating which Is what I'm choosing to focus on considering I invited him over for dinner.

Two adults just catching up and having dinner.

The front doorbell rings and I stand up, straightening out my sweats and hoodie. I chose comfort today and almost every day that I don't work. Since exams were happening I had the week off from work which was a blessing in disguise. I think I'd take the rush of the hospital and long hours over the panic of studying anyway.

"Hey," I greet Mason.

He smiles and I move over letting him in. I watch him as he looks around the house. He's wearing dark faded jeans and a jacket over a long sleeve black shirt. His arm is still in the sling and I remind myself to ask him how much longer that's going to be. Even though he's dressed casually he still drives my head wild.

"Your Dad home?" When he turns to look at me I clear my throat and step around him.

"No, he's out meeting some friends. Thought it'd be good for him to get out of the house." I push my notebooks off the couch giving him a place to sit.

I wouldn't call our living room small, but it wasn't nearly the size of Masons' own house. The moment he enters it though, it feels as though we've entered Alice in Wonderland and taken a bite of the "eat me" cake. His presence fills up the room and reminds me of just how much of an impact he has on a space.

All six feet and five inches of him.

"We never really talked about your mother and how your father's doing. We don't have to if you don't want to, but I'd like to hear it." The couch dips from his weight and he leans forward resting his elbow on his knee.

We're sitting on opposite ends of the couch and I find myself wanting to move closer to the heat of his body, but I don't.

Friends remember.

"Maybe another time." I try to smile. "I've had enough depressing talks this past month that will last me a lifetime." I reach forward, taking a sip from my water bottle. I feel his eyes follow my movements, dropping to my lips when I drink.

I gulp.

"Yea, yea." He clears his throat.

I wonder if being back in my house is weird for him, like the first time I visited his home. Like coming back to a place that was as familiar as the back of your hand but now different and forgotten.

I watch him look around, taking in the living room. He scans the pictures on the walls and the frames on the side tables. He stops on one of my father, mom, and me before looking away.

I remember the first time he told me about his own mother, and what had happened to her. I remember the devastation and guilt he held from it. I consistently told him nothing was his fault, and that he is not to blame for his mother's actions. Her choices were hers, her own mind working against her.

"Big test?" He grins, pointing to my stack of books.

"Unfortunately. I have exams coming up." A reminder of how little I've actually been studying but it doesn't matter, that was another day's problem. This moment's own problem was how I was going to get through this night, with my friend.

"I still can't believe you're going to be a PA. I remember how excited you were, all the hours you racked up in college while still going to class. Determined, like always." He speaks with admiration and I feel the heat rise to my cheeks.

"No need to butter me up Mason, you're already in my house." I joke but he just grins, eyes never leaving mine. The air around us grows thick and my gaze drops to his mouth before I turn away clearing my throat.

"I am, aren't I." He swallows. "Why am I?" He gazes at me accusingly but his lips pull up in a smirk as if to say, what am I really doing here? I've been asking myself that same question all afternoon since I texted him inviting him over, coming up with no real answer.

I shrug. "To eat dinner with a friend."

He looks at me like he sees right through me so I reach for the takeout menus under the coffee table and toss them on his lap.

"You choose." The small pamphlets land on his lap and he clenches his jaw. Both of us keep eye contact, in a silent battle of who's going to break through the tape first. Which one of us is going to cross that line, and bring the other one with us?

It wouldn't be, it couldn't be. We were friends once before we dated, we just had to navigate that normal again. At least for the limited time, he planned on staying here, which is the biggest blinking red light on why this is all deep down a really bad idea.

He doesn't say anything else for a moment but then shuffles through the menus settling on a Thai place in town. We both come up with our order and he calls it in. I find myself staring at his hand as he talks, his narrow veins running up his forearm whenever he moves on the call. Million-dollar hands, hands that I knew well.

I need water.

"It'll be delivered in twenty. Want to watch a movie?" I nod my head and pray to anyone who is listening to remind me why we broke up in the first place, why I shouldn't just be the one to break the line.

I wondered, for a split second, if what my Dad had said at the restaurant was true. That we were meant to find one another again, that this was a second chance. And I was afraid, so afraid because it got harder each time we were in a room together to say what we both bite our tongues from saying.

"Here." He hands me the remote, making himself comfortable. I reach for the blanket behind the couch, settling on the other end and draping it over me. I look over to him once more before turning towards the random movie I settled on, wondering if these twenty minutes until the food gets here will go by fast.

It doesn't.

It feels like for twenty minutes I was hyper-aware of every little movement he made, every shift in position. I don't even know the plot of the movie we're watching and I don't think I really care. We settle around the kitchen island to eat, talking about our favorite dishes and what we miss about food in our college town.

He lights up when talking about college, his old friends, and his old routines. I'm sure he's been on a whirlwind of change since graduation and it was nice to settle into some familiarity. At least a semblance of it.

"You remember that one night you were craving a cheese pizza from Franks? And it was like two am in the morning." He says, dropping his fork and looking up at me with a smile. "You had been out with your friends that night and I had to pick you up after one too many rounds of green tea shots." He points a finger at me.

I shake my head. "I do remember that, but I also remember you making me an awful version of my favorite pizza instead." Memories of that night come flying back, a random thirsty Thursday with my friends from class turned into a night at the bar. All the pizza places around us had closed including Franks. Which I'm guessing is when Mason decided he was going to be a Michelin-rated chef and make me a pizza from scratch.

"Hey! You weren't complaining then. You told me I was the best person ever," he mimics me in a fake drunk voice. "And then you kept me up until five am, making practice the next morning impossible." He ducks his head, both of us knowing why we were up until five am.

His lips on mine, skin on skin. His head between my legs and my hands tugging at his hair–all glimpses of why.

"It's not like you ever got up on time for practice anyway." I joke, hoping to change the subject.

"You made it too hard." He replies, successfully not changing the subject. I look up at him from across the table, his hair is a mess and I'm feeling like we are no longer talking as friends, something he loves to do.

"Stop trying to flirt with me, Mason," I say with a hint of sarcasm, but I mean it. If he continues talking and looking at me the way he does, I'm afraid my heart won't make it out. The distinction between where I'm supposed to stay versus not crossing becomes blurry.

He stands to his full height eyes on me and breathing a bit heavier than he was before. I hold my own breath when he makes his way around the table to stand next to me. He's inches apart and I'm wondering if he can see the stain on my sweatpants from earlier or the acne scars on my forehead. I wonder if he's thinking the same thoughts or ones that will get us in trouble.

"I wouldn't have to try Del." Lifting a finger, I watch as he brushes a piece of my red hair away from my face leaving me breathless. "We never really talked about our kiss." He crosses his arms and leans a hip on the island. Wanting to be at a more fair advantage I stand up straight, mirroring his body.

"There's nothing to talk about." I look away. "It was just a kiss, a lapse in judgment like I said." I try to sound convincing, just like I've been doing in my own head for the last week or so since it happened.

"Is that what you think? Or is that what you're telling yourself?" I feel him step closer, so close I can smell his unfamiliar cologne and the thought makes me sad. I wonder if he still wears the one I used to love, the one I'd buy for him on Christmas or his birthday.

It doesn't matter.

"I meant it when I said I wasn't sorry. I meant it when I said that I should've done it sooner. If you had let me." He leans in and I finally turn to him trying to stay strong, resisting him.

"Answer me this, why did you invite me over for dinner? Just the two of us? And don't give me the friend bullshit, I know you, Delilah. I know us. This means something." He clenches his jaw and I watch his eyes frantically scan my face for me to give him anything. I don't think so, and I find the hem of his shirt on his neck more interesting than eye contact.

"Stop. Don't, okay? Let's just go back to the movie." I step away from the island but don't get far before Mason is whipping his body around to reach for my arm with his left hand. Stopping I turn to him ready to rip my arm away but I don't.

"When you are ready to stop pretending to yourself, I'll be here. You can't get rid of me Delilah. I walked away once before because that's what we both agreed was best, I won't walk away again. At least not without a solid answer this time." I think I need to lie down.

He's got a grip on my arm and an even stronger hold on my heart. I want to go back to two months ago and not agree to dinner with him again. I want to go back and change the trajectory of our lives so that we wouldn't be here in these situations.

"I'm not lying to myself, Mason. I'm not lying to you. I've been upfront with you from the beginning, I'm not going down that road again." I step back, freeing my arm from his grasp. He drops his grip and clenches his jaw. "I care about you, there is no secret there. I want to be friends with you, I want you to feel less alone throughout all of this but us? We can't." I breathe out, finishing my mini rant.

He looks at me seriously, his brows furrowed in concentration. I watch as different emotions pass through his eyes. I prepare myself for him to keep going, to keep pressuring me into an answer he knows is the truth. He could always read me, read right past what I was hiding.

"Okay. Fine, just friends." He says friends like it's a bite of venom but he nods and backs away. "I'll head home. Don't worry about paying me for the Thai, my treat." He reaches for the money I left on the table for him and places it in my hand.

I don't say anything more as he gets his things together and leaves, the door closing shut behind him. If studying all day was not one to bring a full-fledged headache out, that conversation definitely was. I slide down my island, back to the cool wood, and drop my head into my arms.

I was scared and a coward. I know deep down that there was more to it than that, but from what I could scrap our very encounter we've had—I'm scared.

I lost him once, then right after lost my own mother. I didn't want to lose anyone else and in order to do that, I couldn't gain anyone. It's how it had to be for my own sake, my own well being.

I think I deserve a glass of wine.

22 - Mason

"Look who finally came up to visit." Shawn's boisterous voice fills the air the second I close the door to his flashy apartment.

Since the team had successfully secured the AFC championship they had some time off before the big game. When he and Darius had texted asking if I wanted to come up and hang with them and see the rest of the team, I had wanted to say no.

I fronted that I was handling being out of work as best I could, but seeing them may just be something I wasn't ready for. Seeing the whole team thriving and doing just fine without me would send my mind into a panic. Especially after the phone call with my manager.

"Shut up dickhead." I slap the back of Shawn's neck and give Darius a quick half-hug who stands by the small bar cart. "Shawn. You make millions of dollars, why do you have the world's smallest bar cart?" Darius lifts up the different bottles in disgust. You'd think being men in their late twenties almost thirties that they'd care less about a fucking bar cart.

Not these two idiots.

"I don't care what it is, pour me something straight," I say, sitting down beside Shawn in the living room. He slaps my good shoulder to which I shove him off and lean forward.

"I'm glad you came up. I just wish you wanted to go out." He frowns like his puppy was just kicked. He's an active member of a football team who is going to the Superbowl and thinks that going out drinking is on the list of approved activities.

I wonder sometimes if he actually had a brain.

"Do you choose to be an idiot? If the coach saw you out right now you'd be benched. Done." Darius reads my mind, handing me a glass of bourbon and taking a seat across from us on a plush chair. "This is as much fun as we're having right now. After we get that big win though? I don't care about being sober ever again." I watch as Darius lifts his glass and I follow suit in a silent cheer.

It kind of feels as though I'm on the sidelines of my own life, hearing them talk about the game and winning, knowing I won't be there. At least not on the field.

"So, pretty boy." I roll my eyes at Shawn's nickname for me, one I've punched him over several times. "How's Delilah? After the bar that night, I was sure you'd be a thing now."

Delilah. I wanted to forget about our recent exchange, which Is why I found myself here.

I had to stop his wishful thinking. After last night, I was done pretending like there was hope. She gave me her answer, I had to accept that. I'd do my impossible best impression at being a friend. That's all I could get.

"Just friends. She's got a lot of shit going on with school and I'm moving back soon. It wouldn't work." I brush off the seriousness of it all with a shrug of my shoulders and a sip of my drink. "What about you Shawn? Finally settling down?" I knew the answer before he even attempted to reply. He was almost allergic to commitment, always off with someone new.

He likes to put on an act though, I think there is a lot more depth to him than he lets on.

"Absolutely not." He knocks back a shot and smiles wide. "Although watching you two be whipped by two beautiful women has forced me into reconsidering the thought." I roll my eyes.

"I'm not whipped," I say.

Both Darius and Shawn turn to me, look me dead in the eye, then look at one another and laugh. As if the world's funniest comedian was in the room, they laugh, some secret conversation going on between them that I'm unaware of.

"Both of you suck." I stand up, flipping them off before making my way to the bathroom. If they want to be assholes and think something, then so be it. I'll just have to prove them otherwise, prove myself otherwise.

What Delilah and I had was over.

Over.

—-

"Dude, I am never drinking again." Shawn rolls off the side of the couch, squinting at the bright light that feeds in through the blind-free windows. I rack my brain for where I am for a moment, looking around and swallowing back the feeling of nausea in my gut.

I look down at where I lay on a very cramped living room chair. I must've fallen asleep sitting up, not bothering to head down the hall to the guest bedroom. Apparently, Shawn didn't either.

"Good to see you two idiots are up." Darius filters in from the kitchen holding two water bottles. He tosses me on his way over to Shawn. I squint my eyes and groan into my hand, a migraine already spreading across the back of my eyes. Hangover migraines were the absolute worst.

"Shut up, please." I groan, leaning back to put my arm over my eyes. I gulp back half the bottle of water before speaking again. "What happened?" I lean forward, finally looking up to Shawn who is spread out on the floor still, and then to Darius who leans against the frame of the living room entryway sipping on a hot cup of coffee.

"Shawn happened. Convinced to play a drinking game, you were hellbent on proving that you were over Delilah. He said a girl's name and you'd have to message her on Instagram or take a shot." Darius takes a seat, pointing to me. "Let's just say you took a lot of shots." He laughs, and I sigh.

What a fucking stupid game. A game both of them knew I'd lose, I barely even had a game anymore never mind the guts to hit up random girls.

"Wait, but how is he fucked?" I nod to the rolling wide receiver on the ground.

"He matched you." Darius shrugs and Shawn grunts.

I ignore them both, done with the mistakes of last night. I sit up and promise to never drink again, just like Shawn's pained voice groaned out earlier. I head to the shower and erase the night away, scrubbing away the alcohol seeping through my pores.

I find myself in the kitchen twenty minutes later, the three of us eating some shitty toast and eggs in silence. I think Shawn is even still a little drunk from this morning and I worry he may never recover from this. Darius and I both laugh at his attempt to swallow the food, then both of us turn away when he darts for the bathroom, holding his mouth.

"He's still the same," I comment, moving to sit at the island bar seat.

"You want to talk about last night?" Darius takes a seat next to me, nudging my left shoulder. I shrug, not really wanting to spill. I don't remember much and from what I do I can't help but be embarrassed.

"Nah." I take a sip of the hot coffee I poured for myself, wincing as the scorching liquid touches my tongue but welcoming the shock.

"Alright. Should we talk about the Warriors then?" He asks.

"Ugh," I groan and roll my head. "Why are you all for hard conversations so early in the morning?" I look over at him and glare.

"Because I barely hear from you anymore and I'm worried bro. It's not like you to not talk to us. Plus, I know if I was out I'd be spiraling, definitely not okay." His dark eyebrows scrunch in concern and I turn away.

"Well, I guess we can talk about the fact my Ma reached out to my Dad. For more money." I say casually, not wanting to make a big deal. Darius chokes on his sip of coffee and I roll my eyes.

"Talk about big conversations, that's a big one Mas. Shit." His voice strained from the choking.

"It's not big if we don't make it big." I divert his concern.

We could be talking shit about Shawn, that would be a light conversation. Or about how New York's team lost the playoff seed once again, we always did love talking about that. Or I could annoy him about his secret love for the Bridgerton show on Netflix.

He claims he only watches it around his wife, but I've seen him secretly pulling it out on away games. Busted.

"That's big Mason. When's the last time you've heard from her?" He asks.

"I don't know, awhile. I can't say I'm surprised that she reached out again. It was only a matter of time." I think about the last time I heard from her and come up blank. I can't help but put up walls against her, for my own good.

"Did she check on you?" He leans forward on the island.

"No." I bite out.

It was delusional for me to assume she would in the first place, delusional to even have hope. She made her decision long ago on what she valued most in her life, and until she decided against that, she would never get better.

"I'm sorry, Bro." Darius sighs and I nod.

"It's fine. Not your fault." I stand, bringing my empty plate to the sink. "It's not like my Dad is going to give anything to her. Not again, not after she spent it all last time." I rinse my dish, ignoring the sting of my own words.

Addiction is a cruel thing for both the addict and the family of them,

"And what do you think? What would you do?" Darius drills me further.

I think about it for a moment, wondering what I would do in my Dad's place. He may have built up even stronger walls than my own, fortifying her out of his life and moving on. But a small part of me knows I can never fully do that, she will always be my mother, sober or not. I'll always struggle with both the devil and the angel on my shoulders when it comes to her.

"If I'm being completely honest, I don't know," I answer.

I dry the dish after cleaning it and place it on the dish mat. I figure dirty dishes will be the last thing on Shawn's mind today.

"Well, what if you try and see her?" He clears his throat and I freeze.

"No," I answer right away, not entertaining the idea.

"Listen to me, Mason." I hear him stand and walk up next to me. I move away, allowing him to wash his own dish, finding the cabinet more entertaining. I massage my right shoulder gently, it's already in a sore state, unhappy about sleeping in a chair the night before.

"It may be worth just trying. Maybe this time it will be different, and if it's not you can tell yourself you've tried." I hear the words he speaks but ignore what he says.

"With addicts, it's never different D. I've told you this." I don't mean to snap but I do, feeling overwhelmed by the conversation.

"Just think about it. No harm in that." Darius says and then turns to leave down the hall.

Once I'm alone I lean my hand on the counter and take a deep breath. I couldn't actually be considering this, considering seeing her. I'm injured, I'm supposed to be resting and keeping my life as stress-free as possible. This idea is anything but that.

But I can't help thinking of the what ifs, the what could be.

This may be why when I leave the apartment after saying goodbye to them both, later that day, I pull out the crumpled piece of paper I shoved in the back of the pair of jeans I was wearing that day in my father's office.

112 Harding Way

Laconic NH, 02134

$5,000 ... please.

I stare at the please and then the address before climbing into the car waiting for me out front.

23 - Mason

The ever-changing weather of the east coast sends a shock to my system each morning. The past two weeks have been unforgivingly cold and now it was comfortable enough to leave the house without a jacket. This time of year the weather always delivers whiplash, not knowing if in the morning we'd need a snowsuit and at night a bathing suit.

Today it was closer to shorts with a warmish fifty-five degrees.

I had gotten back from Boston last night around dinner time, walking into Marie and my Dad at the table. It seems like they're good again, the both of them even laughing at something they were talking about. I still didn't fully trust my dad and his back-and-forth behavior, but for Marie, I was glad he at least was treating his wife with basic respect.

I thank my uber driver before stepping out to the front of the Hospital. Today was the day my sling would be taken off and I was restless since the sound of my alarm at eight am this morning. I was itching to get rid of it completely, impatient to get my stiff shoulder and elbow extended.

I knew the routine by now—the floor to find and the waiting room to mindlessly spend thirty minutes waiting in. I shot both Darius and Shawn a text about the appointment.

Shawn: Selfie with your arm free or it didn't HAPPEN!

I roll my eyes at his reply and close my phone.

I couldn't believe that it had already been a little over a month since the initial injury. Sometimes, in my dreams, I still felt the phantom pain of the opposing player crashing into me. The shock of hitting the ground and knowing something was wrong. It all felt like a messed up dream, one I was tired of living in.

"Mason." A nurse calls me to the back, Linda, who's been the nurse to bring me back each time. She's got gray hair and stress lines littering her face but she's always got the warmest smile. Young and refreshing each visit.

I'm normally impatient with these visits but today is worse. Dr. Karr enters the room, going over the usual initial pain assessment and prognosis updates. I answer all her questions routinely, and extra quickly. By the end of the visit, I smile at the release of the sling's snap and the weight of it being gone both physically and metaphorically is uplifting.

Dr. Karr rattles off the rules and how to keep my arm safe through recovery. She smiles throughout it, clearly feeding off of my own happiness. I still am very restricted with my movements and need to wear the sling whenever I feel pain or am going to be doing strenuous activity.

Seems easy enough to me.

I flex the fingers of my right hand, stepping out of the hospital. The stitches where my surgical incision was are healing up nicely, and the feeling of extending and flexing my arm slowly is victorious.

I can't explain it, but it sends a shrill down my spine like I can picture the grip of a football in my aching fingers.

"Well, well, well." I turn to the voice to my left. "If he isn't home free." Delilah smiles and points to my sling-free arm. I scan her body, unconsciously taking in the emerald green scrubs she wears and how it fit with her red hair so well. Her hips flare out and I force myself to look up at her face.

She smiles.

"I mean what can I say," I laugh and pull up my arm to pretend to flex. I still don't have much range of motion and there is a trail of pain with the curling movement, but I don't care.

"Careful now, they'll send you right back into that sling." Her laughter is clear through the unusually warm air. Like myself, she ditched the heavy winter coat today, wearing a light gray jacket over her scrubs.

Scrubs that fit her too well.

Focus.

"Are you heading to work?" What a dumb question, but of course she is.

She nods before answering. "Yea, working a mid-shift today. It shouldn't be too bad. I have a friend on shift and a home-cooked meal." She nods to the lunchbox hanging low in her hand. I watch, mesmerized, as she pulls her long red hair over one shoulder. I hone in on the exposed skin of her neck, wishing I could pull her close and kiss her right on her pulse line.

One I knew she loved.

She looks up at me, noticing my staring and a faint blush coats her cheeks. I know she feels the tension between us both, it's palpable each time we're together. After our last encounter, I solidified that she's just a friend, one rule she consistently reinforced—but my head and heart had a hard time following.

"That's cool. You're almost done with your program?" I ask her another question, not wanting the conversation to end. I'd ask her every question under the sun that I already knew the answer too if it meant I got to watch her smile and her eyes light up as she talks.

She's just so beautiful.

"Yea, almost. A couple more months." Excitement swirls in her eyes and I smile. "That's awesome Del, I'm sure you can't wait to graduate." I eye her reaction.

"Oh, you have no idea. It's been way too long. I think when I walk across that stage I'll feel the weight of the world lift from my shoulders." She laughs and steps to the side as someone walks behind her. "It will be a great day." Her words are formal and responses are expected, but the way her eyes wander to my chest and the dart of her tongue over her lips—I know she feels it too.

I told her about how I went to Boston for the weekend to see my friends. She asks about them both, nodding and laughing when I tell her about Shawn's night. She asks if I plan to go back anytime soon, and both of us feel the weight of her question as it leaves her lips.

"Um, I'm not really sure," I answer honestly. "There is something I have to do before I make any decisions on moving back. Not to mention I probably have no control over it with the team, I assume the coach and the medical staff have a game plan." One that I haven't heard yet, one I'm sure I'd plan out soon with the news of my sling removal and start of physical therapy.

"I see. Anything serious you have to do?" She rolls her lips and looks at me seriously. She always could read me, as I did her. Knowing that the something I had to do, dampened my mood.

I think about it for a moment and then before I give myself time to back out, the words are flying out of my mouth.

"My mom. She reached out again and I think I'm going to go see her." I say, watching her eyes drop and her mouth curve downward. Of course, she knew of the struggle with my mom, the battle she fought daily. She was there through moments of weakness, there when I wished my mother would call me for the simplest things like a birthday. She was just there.

"Oh, Mason." She sighs and looks up. "Is she better?" I see it in her eyes, the answer to her question like she knows the inevitable.

"No." She nods at my confirmation. "She's somewhere up in New Hampshire." I look down and grab the back of my neck, the topic sending stress to my head. "I just think I need to do this. See her, one last time or one more time." I voice my thoughts, comfortable enough at telling her this.

She nods, stepping forward. Her hand reaches up to rub my arm in a soothing gesture.

"I'm glad you've gotten in contact. Maybe this will be good for you." She says reassuringly.

I highly doubt anything about going to see my mom will be good for me, but I know It's something I need to do. I've been away, avoiding my problems on the road and in my career bubble. The rocky relationship with my dad allowed me to avoid any serious conversations about family, like the one with my mother.

I reach for Delilah's hand, not missing the way her breath catches and her eyes flash to mine. I hold her gaze as my fingers wrap around her own, slowly bringing them down between us. I squeeze the grip and smile.

We both allow the moment to pass and then some before I'm pulling away.

Just friends.

It's awkward for a moment, her gaze on the ground and my chest swelling with something along the lines of yearning.

"Want to do something for me, as a friend?" I ask about making another dumb decision. She nods her head, eyes questioning. "Want to come with me?" I watch her reaction, hoping it doesn't backfire in my face.

Her eyebrows shoot up and she's making that face she always does when her mind is racing. It's cute, just like her attempt to hide the fact she won't jump on the opportunity to be with me if she could.

We both know this.

"It will be this weekend. We'll leave Saturday, and be back Sunday night." I tell her, knowing she probably has to work the week, just hoping she's got the weekend off.

"Yea, yea sure. If you need me, I'll be there for you." She finally meets my eyes. "I have to clock in now but text me the details and the plan." She clears her throat and diverts her attention to the door.

"Okay. Thank you, Del. Means a lot." I say, watching her lookup once more. She just smiles before making her way into the hospital. My eyes follow her retreating form and my heart starts beating a little faster at the idea of a weekend away with her.

Just the two of us, confronting the present with the past my my side.

Surely everything would be okay.

Just friends, right?

24 - Delilah

"Call me if you need anything, I mean anything. I left some pre-made dinners in the fridge along with Clara's number on the door if there is an emergency." I shuffle through my mental checklist of things I need to tell Dad before leaving.

Mason texted letting me know he was on the way—with a driver.

Apparently, a driver was in the budget of things he needed these days due to his shoulder injury and limited motion. It made sense why he couldn't drive, but I wouldn't tease him any less about it when I got the chance.

"I'll be fine Delilah. Just go have fun, the both of you." My Dad smirks and wiggles his eyebrows, to which I just roll my eyes. "I told you, I'm just going to help him find his Mom." I point to him, "as a friend." He just laughs.

It seems as though no one has confidence in me. When I told Clara and Ryan they both exchanged knowing glances and before I knew it they were laughing. I flipped them off and reminded myself that I know what I'm doing and didn't need their approval.

Then I received a text from Tish.

Tish: Can't wait for the hookup story when you get back!

No one had hope in me.

"Sure sweetie, now come here and give me a hug." The sound of a horn followed by the ding of a text confirmed Mason's arrival. I walk over to my Dad, hugging him tightly. I know he's been better lately, and that therapy has been consistent, but I'm still worried. Worried that he'd spiral when I wasn't here or wasn't close by to help him. Both Clara and Ryan offered to help, both of them knowing exactly the extent of my Dad's mental state.

"Love you," I mumble into his warm chest, pulling away. "Don't burn the house down while I'm gone." Fixing the strap of my overnight bag, I swing my backpack on as well. I was a chronic over-packer, with my backpack carrying all my electronics just in case of an emergency quiz or exam—and my overnight bag stuffed to the brim with "what if?" outfits.

What if we go to dinner? What if the hotel has a pool? What if we go snowboarding?

I had to be prepared.

"Love you too, now go before he leaves." My Dad helps me to the front door, opening it for me. Waiting outside in my driveway is a black SUV that dwarfs the asphalt, making my driveway look tiny. Mason leaned against the car and for a moment I forgot how to breathe. Black sunglasses frame his face along with a New England Warriors ball cap. He wears a black hoodie and heather gray sweatpants. I force myself not to drop my eyes below the waist of his drawstring sweats.

I was going to hell.

"There you are. Thought I'd have to send a search party." Mason teases, lifting his glasses off his face. I put my best-unbothered appearance forward. "No need. I'm here." I tease, shrugging my shoulders full of stuff.

"That you are. Along with enough stuff for two weeks. Did I send you the right plans? You know we're only away for one night?" Mason teases, reaching with his left arm and nursing his right close to his body, for the strap of my bag. I let him take it, watching as he flinches at the weight.

"Jesus, Del." He swears under his breath and I roll my eyes.

"You're really out of shape if you think that's heavy, Jones." I smile at his retreating form towards the trunk of the car. The driver gets out to open the trunk, letting Mason drop my bag in the back next to his.

Mason laughs at my response, making his way back over to where I stand gripping my backpack to avoid fidgeting.

"Oh Del girl. You and I both know I'm not out of shape." He drops his head, tilting it to catch my gaze. "Isn't that right?" He says with a knowing smirk.

I take back what I was saying earlier, everyone was right. I'd never make it through this trip, not with the way he was looking at me like we were not just friends. Not by the way each word leaving his mouth was laced with underlying desire.

"Cocky much." I tilt my head, ignoring my body's reaction.

"Only for you." He laughs, moving to open the car door. "Now let's go, we're already running behind schedule." He teases, alluding that I took too long. I just flip him off and turn to face my Dad who stands on the porch with a knowing look. I wave to him goodbye and he waves back, wearing a smirk on his aging face.

Mason turns to where I wave.

"I'll take good care of her Mr. McKenna," Mason shouts over the lawn and pulls his glasses down.

"Oh, I know you will, boy!" My Dad shouts back and I almost reel in embarrassment. Could both of them not be any more obvious?

Mason waves once more and then closes the door. I take a breath, preparing myself for the drive. The door to my right opens, and I furrow my brow as Mason shuffles in the back with me.

"Are you not sitting up front?" I ask a little too quickly, nerves seeping through. I could take a car ride with him, possibly get through it while he sits up front and me in the back. But the two of us, here in the back with barely a middle seat between us?

Regrets enter my thoughts.

"And leave you back here alone, Del? What kind of friend would that make me?" He fakes hurt, slapping his left hand to his chest in shock. I can't help the laugh that comes out of my lips, watching him wince at his actions.

"Serves you right," I whisper under my breath, turning to put my seatbelt on.

"You're being a really mean friend right now," Mason says, using the word friend every chance he gets like a slap in the face. Like he knows that I know, friendship is the last relationship the both of us tread on.

Lord help me.

—

"You're telling me you'd rather be an astronaut and go to space than explore the deep ocean?" Mason asks dead serious, our game of existential life questions going too far. I hide my laugh at how serious he is, knowing I was just joking most of the time.

"Yea. Space is terrifying but so cool." I point out.

"But don't you want to know what's on this planet before exploring others?" He asks, gaze hardened on mine.

"I don't actually. I'm good with never knowing what's at the bottom of the ocean so long as it stays down there." I tease, liking the way he furrows his brows and licks at his lips.

"You can say the same for space!" He shouts, shaking his head. At the sound of my laughter, he shakes his head and turns to look out the window. "You're bad at this game." He grunts out and I cover my mouth at how hard I want to laugh.

So serious, so cute.

"Sorry," I say, not really apologetic because seeing him so concentrated was kind of hot. I forgot the feeling of being on the receiving end of a Mason debate. He put his whole body into whatever he was feeling and arguing. Zoned and locked into winning or proving someone wrong.

"Mhm." He says, turning to look at me with a teasing smile. "You used to love doing that. Getting me all heated just to say you're joking, or agree with me." He says it casually but the weight of, used to, is like a knife to the gut.

"Sure did." I smile back. "Are you nervous?" We're only about thirty minutes from the address Mason's mom had given his Dad. I noticed throughout our game he became more fidgety, from the flexing of his forearm as he twirled his sunglasses to the lifting and re-placing of his ball cap—he's nervous.

"Yea. Kind of." He answers honestly. "I can say I don't know what to expect but I'm not naive. She'll most likely be high, or not herself. I've just been mentally preparing to see that." He furrows his brows, looking down at his clasped fingers.

I feel for him. Not knowing how your own parents will react to seeing you have to be so hard. Has to be another type of pain, a pain I wish I could take away from him.

"Well, like my own mother used to say, you won't know if you don't try. Which she definitely got from literally everyone else because I've heard that saying since I was a girl." I try to lighten the mood with a laugh but at the mention of my own mother a cloud of grief hangs over my heart.

Mason looks up, a small sad smile on his perfect face.

"Was she happy? Before you know... before she died?" He asks softly but the blow is hard. I know I owe him some explanation, I owe him answers for what happened. It's been years and I should be able to talk about it more freely now. But nothing heals the gaping wound of losing a parent.

"Yea. Yea she was." I smile down at my fingers, playing with the belt of my jeans. "She got sick and depleted pretty quickly. Stage four lung cancer." I say, answering the question I know was plaguing his mind.

"It's funny because she never smoked a day in her life. She was healthy and always happy. Then over time, she began to have shortness of breath and frequent chest pains, so we made her an appointment." I feel a tear drop from my cheek and wipe it away.

Remembering the phone call I got from her while at my part-time job. The pain in her voice when she told me I needed to come home, that they had to tell me something. I'll never forget the sound of my father breaking down that night, the night we all grieved in our own rooms. Grieved for the inevitable.

"I'm so fucking sorry, Del." Mason reaches over, brushing my hair from my face and squeezing my shoulder. I look up and smile, swallowing back any tears.

"But yes, she was happy. We surrounded her with as much love as we could give. Making every night and every day worth it." I say.

His green eyes find mine and we both share a moment of silence, lost in a gaze. His hand still cups the back of my shoulder and the warmth of it spreads throughout my body. He seems to notice my attention has zeroed in on his hand and he drops it, dragging it slowly down my back.

The both of us take a breath before I break eye contact.

"We're five minutes out, Mason." Our driver announcements.

I look out the window watching the endless trees whizz by. The address was in a heavily wooded area, not unlike all the other properties here in New Hampshire. A fresh coat of snow lined the ground, the sun out.

I hoped, for Mason's sake, that this visit went smoothly. That he'd get the answers to his questions or whatever he had in mind for today.

I hoped for his sake, his Mother would be there for him.

25 - Mason

"Want me to knock for you?"

Delilah stands behind me, her presence made known by the flap of her hair on her winter coat. We arrived at the address just minutes ago, I took a minute to breathe it out in the car before having the guts to actually get out.

I look up at the chipped shingles of the three-story home. There's no light shining through the dirty windows and even a few side shutters hang off their hinges. The thought of my mother living here, alone, while I sit comfortably in a high-rise apartment in the city sends traitors' guilt through me. I knew she couldn't have been off well, I knew that she wasn't living the best life. But actually seeing it makes me sick.

"No," I answered Del's question. "I'm good." I step forward and knock my left fist on the door. There's no doorbell from what I can see, so I knock a couple of times and hope there's someone home.

I stand back, waiting.

Delilah doesn't say anything and neither do I. Both of us were probably thinking the same thing, wondering if she was really here or if this was another scam somehow. But, before I can let my mind wander, footsteps are heard from inside.

I swallow and tighten my hands into a fist, bracing myself. The sounds of clicking from a lock being undone is loud enough to hear. I step back into Delilah, wanting to shield her body with mine. She wordlessly pushes her arm around my left, gripping it reassuringly.

The door slams open, and standing on the threshold is my mother.

Or, someone who resembles her.

I rake my eyes down her frail body, the sweatpants, and shirt she wears hang loosely over her frail state. I look up at her face, eyes sunken in and pupils large enough to fill her green irises—ones that look strikingly similar to mine.

"Mason?" My mother's shocked voice snaps me back to the present. "Oh my god, baby. I didn't expect to see you!" She launches herself forward and before I can resist she's throwing her arms over my shoulders. I stiffen and force myself to relax, her touch making me uneasy on top of the anxiety that already clings to my nerves.

Delilah moves back but doesn't drop her arm, squeezing even tighter. I mentally thank her for it.

"Hi, mom," I say, reluctantly bringing my healing arm to tap her on the back. She steps away, and I drop my arm. She scans me from head to toe, eyes wide like she can't believe I'm actually standing here. I watch her realize we're not alone when her gaze lands on the body behind me.

I clear my throat and divert her attention back to me, not wanting Delilah to get too involved.

"It's so good to see you, baby boy. You're so grown." She marvels at my size, h and races out to squeeze my bicep. I ignore it and step aside.

"I got your note," I say, getting straight to the point already feeling uncomfortable with being her. I watch her face drop as if she's remembering reality. Yea mom, I'm here because I got your note asking for more money, more money for the meth, heroin, or whatever is your ball and chain this time.

"Oh. That was meant for your father." She swallows and starts to look around frantically. "Did he uh," she pauses and looks up. "Did he give you something to give me?" Her eyes look up at me full of hope, the happiness of seeing me already clouded by the need for drugs. It makes me sick.

"No. We're not here to give you money. I'm here to take you to lunch, to talk." I say, feeling Delilah squeeze my arm once more in reassurance. "I have a driver waiting. Would you like to come?" I keep my voice level and emotion out of it.

I already see her panic start to fester, watch her look to the ground and pick at her torn shirt. She flashes her eyes to me and then back to Delilah.

"Oh baby, is this your girlfriend? She's so beautiful, Mason." She smiles, changing the subject. I feel Delilah step closer to me and I pull her to my side carefully.

"Would you like to get lunch, Lucie?" Delilah's voice is gentle but firm, trying to steer the conversation back to the question at hand. I don't miss the way she dismisses my mother's assumption, not sure how to feel about her not saying yes and not saying no.

My mother sighs and then turns her attention back to me.

"I'm a bit busy today, baby boy. I, I have something," she paces and tosses her hand back to point to the house. "I have something I was doing. I'm uh—" at this point, I stop listening to her excuses as they ramble.

I can't ignore how it hurts. That she wouldn't jump on the opportunity to talk to me again, that she doesn't even want to spend time with me.

It hurts because I know she's hurting.

"Mom, I want to help you," I say, swallowing back the lump in my throat. "Let me help you, I can find you a good rehab Ma. I'll be there for you the best I can, but only if you take that first step." I can tell the words I speak are on deaf ears with her.

She shakes her head.

"Mason baby, I'm okay. I don't need that." She reaches for me again but I step back, forcing Delilah to move with me.

"You do, mom. I know it may seem like what I'm offering is the worst thing imaginable but I promise you the other side is better than what you're going through." I feel my hands shake as I speak. Delilah notices and drops her hand into mine, I grip her palm tightly.

"Well if you want to help, Mason." She gulps. "If you just give me a little money to get by I promise, I swear baby, I'll go to your fancy rehab." I close my eyes as the words leave her lips, predictable but not any less painful.

"I promise, I swear." She steps forward and rests her arm on my shoulder. "Please, Mason." I count to three in my head before stepping away, forcing her arm to drop.

Words are futile in the wake of actions.

"No, mom. I'm sorry." I swallow back what I really want to say.

Why wasn't I enough for you to get better? Do you not realize in going down this road you kill me slowly? I miss my mom, the one who I never got to honestly know. I mourn the loss of someone who stands in front of me, alive.

"Mason, don't be like that." She says, frantically looking between Delilah and I searching for a way to make this go her way. I watch her step toward the direction of the body behind me but I move in front of her path, shielding whatever plea she might force on Del.

"Girl, you have to convince him this is what I need. Do you love him? Convince him his mom needs his help." I almost can't believe the words coming from her lips.

Delilah keeps her grip on my hand, not moving from behind me.

"With all due respect, Lucie, I'm not going to do that." Delilah's voice is calm to my raging heart but I still can't wipe the hurt from the reality of the situation. I don't wait for my mother to reply or for her to try again desperately, I just turn away. My arm finds Delilah's shoulders, bringing her with me.

"Mason, please! You are just like your father!" Anger seeps through my mother's voice and I clench my teeth together to not say anything.

"You're not," Delilah whispers to my side while I open the door for her. I don't see her eyes, I don't look anywhere. I don't want to see her pity or sadness, I just want to get out of here.

Delilah doesn't say a word on our way to the hotel and I mentally thank her for it. I keep my eyes trained on the passing scenery and try to calm my beating heart. I knew what it was going to be like, I knew what was going to happen but I still had hope.

Hope.

Addiction kills hope but doesn't bury it. No matter how many times I find myself thinking of her or wanting to help, just to be disappointed, I just can't seem to shake the strand of wishful thinking. Of hope.

If I could take her pain away I would, I would in a heartbeat. Because that's what it is, pain and regret eased by numbing. In a perfect world, addiction would be easy to treat and help but this world wasn't perfect and never would be.

"Hey, Mason." A hand pats my shoulder and I jump. "We're here." I look over to Delilah who wears a sad smile and nods. She watches me in concern, the concern I want to wipe from her beautiful face. The last thing I'd want is to burden the woman beside me.

We make our way into the lobby of a Holiday Rest, two employees sit at the front desk. It's relatively empty and I'm thankful, not wanting to draw any unnecessary attention. I kept my ball cap on, pulling it down to the crest of my brow bone as I walked up to the front desk. A woman with glasses and freckled skin looks up.

"Hi, how can I help you?" She asks, her gaze flicking from me to Delilah behind me. "I have reservations under the name Jones," I say, feeling a headache start due to the stress of the day. She types something on her computer and then looks up.

"Yep. Jones has one room for one night. If I can just have a credit card for the file, you can be on your way." I look up in surprise. "Uhm, no I booked two rooms." I pinch my brows together just wanting this day to be over.

"Oh, I'm sorry. I can go ahead and get that sorted if you want to take a seat by the doors. I just need to grab my manager for the rebooking." I sigh at her words and turn to apologize to Delilah but she's already stepping up around me, the smell of her comforting perfume filling my nose.

"It's fine." I'm surprised at her words, her face unreadable but I notice she plays with the hem of her jacket a bit. "There are two beds, right? Don't need to make it a hassle, plus you're tired." She looks over to me and offers a smile.

And it's at that moment that I'm overwhelmed with emotion. The only woman I loved was in arms-reach but unreachable. She looks at me like a friend but her heart beats like a lover, her lips parting with slight heavy breathing.

"Yes, there are two beds. Are you sure? I can get that done real quick?" The woman breaks my trance and I look back. "That's fine. We'll take the current room." I give her everything she needs, ignoring the nagging pain behind my eyes and the thumping of my heart. The distance between Delilah and me is suddenly a vortex I can't ignore.

I accepted the key from the employee, thanking her. I turn to face Delilah completely, watching her struggle with the bag she definitely overpacked. She hasn't changed a bit, every loveable part of her shining bright.

This was fucking dangerous territory.

"Give it to me Del," I smirk, lifting the bag while hearing her groan in resistance. "I can carry my own, plus you need to be careful of your shoulder." She crosses her arms and my eyes drop to her chest before I turn around quickly.

"I'm just so out of shape, I need the help." I tease, using her own fake insult from earlier. The both of us know I'm nowhere near out of shape, not by the way her own gaze falls on my arms or chest far too often for her to call me out of shape.

We walk silently down the hall, our room on the first floor. We pass a small bar with some people scattered, one I'll definitely be soliciting before the night is over. The minor distraction Delilah offered was not enough to get rid of the ache my mother left behind.

Opening the door to the room, I see two beds. I take the one closest to the door and she takes the one on the far end. I watch her briefly, watching as she settles her things to the corner and even replaces the pillow cover with a pink satin one she pulled from her bag.

"Please tell me you don't still change hotel pillowcases." I drop my own bag onto my bed and take a seat, watching a smile creep up on her face.

"It's been a few years, Mason. I didn't get hit on the head and forget my routines." She teases and I want to soak up the small laugh that bubbles from her mouth.

Our beds are inches apart, the space between us more metaphorical than physical. I allow myself one more moment of remembering before standing and clearing my throat.

"I'm going to head down to the bar for a little. Just text me if you need anything." I tell her, watching as she stops what she's doing.

"Alright." She says, clearing her throat. "Mason, I'm here if you want to talk about it. About today. That's why I came, right?" Her voice is soft and it penetrates right through my walls. I nod and offer her a smile.

I don't want to talk about it. I want to forget about it. So I grab my phone, and the room key, and find the bar from before to settle in for a cold drink.